DATE DUE

		PRINTED IN U.S.A.

Romain Slocom
and photograph

Jesse Browner is

MONSIEUR LE COMMANDANT

ROMAIN SLOCOMBE

Translated from the French
by Jesse Browner

Gallic Books
London

This book is supported by the Institut français du Royaume-Uni
as part of the Burgess programme.

www.frenchbooknews.com

A Gallic Book

First published in France as *Monsieur le Commandant* by éditions NiL, 2011
Copyright © éditions NiL, 2011
English translation copyright © Gallic Books 2013

First published in Great Britain in 2013 by Gallic Books,
59 Ebury Street, London, SW1W 0NZ

A CIP record for this book is available from the British Library
ISBN 978-1-908313-50-8

Typeset in Fournier MT by Gallic Books
Printed and bound by CPI Group (UK) Ltd, Croydon, CR0 4YY

2 4 6 8 10 9 7 5 3 1

To Pascal Garnier

Betrayal can be the fruit of a
superior intelligence, unbound by civic ideologies.

Paul Léautaud,
Passe-temps

FRIENDS OF THE MARÉCHAL

Pledge of Allegiance

I hereby declare that:

I am French, born of a French father and mother;
I am neither a Jew nor a Freemason;
I shall follow Maréchal Pétain in all faith;
I endorse his national and European policy
And am prepared to disseminate and defend that policy,
In the same spirit as Maréchal Pétain, in order to achieve
The active union of all Frenchmen under his leadership.
Surname: Husson
Christian name: Paul-Jean
Profession: Writer, member of the Académie Française
Address: 20 Quai de Verdun, Andigny, Département de l'Eure
I authorise the publication of my pledge for propaganda purposes.

PUBLISHER'S NOTE

The following letter, which comprises the main part of this work, was discovered in May 2006 by the German documentary film-maker Peter Klemm among family papers abandoned in a Leipzig rubbish dump not far from a group of buildings under demolition.

For reasons that will be readily understood, we have deemed it prudent to change the names of the letter-writer, some of the protagonists and a sub-prefecture in Haute-Normandie, as well as that of a literary award and the titles of several books. On the other hand, the occasionally excessive use of capital letters has been retained.

We have also taken the liberty of dividing the manuscript into chapters to make it easier to read.

1.

Herr Sturmbannführer H. Schöllenhammer
Kreiskommandantur
Hôtel de Paris
10 Avenue du Maréchal Pétain
Sous-préfecture d'Andigny, Eure

Villa Némésis
4 September 1942

Monsieur le Commandant,

I should have found it easy, even in a provincial town where everything, or almost everything, becomes common knowledge, to write this letter, which you will receive this evening, anonymously. Yes, forgive me for reiterating this, it should have been easy to remain anonymous.

But anonymity, like mendacity and error – or more particularly, what I consider to be mendacity and error – inspires the most violent revulsion in me. On the threshold of old age, I shall alter neither my opinion on that nor my temperament.

This in no way explains why I permit myself to bore you with a composition that will undoubtedly degenerate gradually into a painful confession; but ever since your arrival in Andigny and the first words exchanged between reserve officer and active duty officer, I have held you in high regard. Despite the differences in our culture and age – I believe I have some twenty years on you – I have sensed that the great distance between us and other people, you by dint of your presence in an occupied land, and I by my remoteness, pure and simple, has somehow created an understanding between us.

I have never indulged in the romantic delusion that writers ought to be saints or heroes to be worshipped at the altar; on the contrary, I believe that the cultivation of such subversive faculties as the imagination and sensibility carries a clear moral risk. That is why so few writers have led exemplary lives.

I was in Paris yesterday, where I called upon Sonderführer[1] Gerhard Heller of the Propagandastaffel.[2] I had requested an urgent meeting with him. When our interview was at an end, I restrained myself with some difficulty – although I had merely to cross the Seine and drive a scant kilometre along half-empty streets – from visiting the one who is always in my thoughts, and who at that hour was most likely still at work in her office at the Opéra.

The Gospel tells us: 'Woe unto him who looks back.'

Holy scripture is clearly speaking here of our devotion to God, which, as I understand it, is absolute and admits of neither reticence nor rejection. One must therefore wipe the slate clean, all or nothing! And having chosen all, having been *compelled* to choose all, I must relinquish all attachment to everything I once desired. When one gives oneself to God, one must give oneself entirely. So it is with all human enterprise. Yet again, I found myself with a choice to make.

I chose.

On the way home, I was alone in the Imperia as it made its swift way along the banks of the Seine. The slope of Rolleboise rose in the distance. Dozing in the drowsy summer warmth, the countryside shone in all its splendour beside the serene river, which was dotted with fishing skiffs and little white wooden houses on stilts, their shutters closed. To my left loomed dark, heavily wooded hills, throwing a shadow across the road that cast my mind back to the terrible events of recent days. Gazing in that direction, I thought of my daughter-in-law. Turning the other way, towards the calm, light-flooded countryside, I recalled the words of Claudel:

> Neither the felicitous plain, nor the harmony of these words, nor the pleasant hue of greenery atop the crimson harvest can satisfy the gaze, which demands light itself. Over there, in that square ditch enclosed by wild mountain walls, the air and the water burn with a mysterious flame. I see gold so beautiful that all of nature seems but a dead mass, and the brightness shed by light itself but the deepest night. Delightful elixir, by what mystic path will it be given me to bathe in your scant waters?

One does not reach the light in a single journey.
One reaches it via a darkling road.

That truth has been amply borne out by three years of war – ever since that 3 September 1939, when the French, having thrown caution to the wind, set off with little enthusiasm in the name of a cause that appeared dubious at best.

All of Europe, a few countries excepted, is now engaged in the hostilities. United by conquest and the spirit of a new world, it is a common bulwark against the enemy in the East. Fourteen months have gone by since your nation, anticipating the imminent onslaught of the Soviets, boldly launched its attack on the boundless Slavic plain. In just a few weeks, you overthrew the enemy's defences, advanced inexorably to the very gates of Moscow and, along a front stretching thousands of kilometres, were able to consolidate your positions before a winter the like of which had not been seen in years. Your offensive resumed this spring: Kerch fell on 15 May, and Sevastopol, the strongest fortress in the world, vainly resisted a hellish siege until 1 July. The Crimea has been conquered. The brave Wehrmacht took Kharkov on 24 May, reached the Don at Voronezh, swept Voroshilovgrad and, having captured Rostov-on-Don on 24 July, occupied the lands either side of the Don before marching off to Stalingrad and the Caucasus!

Never has Stalin been in such peril, and his appeals for an Anglo-American distraction, the so-called 'second front', are growing shriller by the minute. But as you so rightly pointed out to Dr Hild last Sunday, following our game of chess in the gardens of the Bellevue, the British are already mired in a second front in North Africa, where Rommel's armoured divisions have forced Ritchie's Eighth Army into retreat and crossed the Egyptian border.

But let us set all this aside, for you know as well as I do how impossible it is to foretell the end of the gargantuan struggle that is now pitting one half of the world against the other.

That, in short, was what was on my mind on that Normandy road, whose every turn, copse, forest, dale, combe, spire and village I know so well ... My ears picked up the monotonous drone of the engine, the wind whistling through the car window; I breathed in petrol fumes mingled with the musky scent of fields recently harvested, drenched in heat and light, and bathed in smouldering, dreamy languor, like a woman who has just made love. I passed a line of barges slowly pushing upstream, the river sparkling with reflected sunlight, air and water mysteriously aflame. As the road straightened out ahead, I put my foot down. The blood beat savagely in my temples, coursed through my tired veins. I thought of Ilse. Again!

The truth of what had to be done – cruel and blinding like the summer light – struck me.

I *had* to put an end to it.

Woe unto him who looks back.
Such was our woe, our crime, our downfall.

2.

I set my pen aside for a moment and tried to order my thoughts. So that you might understand the reason for my long account – and for certain conversations that I shall later have to transcribe in detail, as well as for certain acts of abject violence – I must go back in time to 1932, the year when Ilse Wolffsohn entered our lives. When I say our lives, I mean mine and those of my wife and two children.

You have met Ilse, Monsieur le Commandant, having once exchanged a few words with her in French – which she speaks perfectly, as she does English and Italian. I introduced her to you that day as 'my daughter-in-law, Madame Olivier Husson', careful to avoid using her German Christian name. That was last year, after Mass one Sunday in autumn, I'm sure you recall. But you have never met my son Olivier. I have never spoken of him to you. You will know why.

My son always had a gift for music. Which is far from the case with me, I'm sorry to say. But God has offered me certain compensations: instead of concertos and symphonies I have my novels and my plays. Olivier first took up the piano at a very tender age, and then switched to the violin. My daughter Jeanne, two years his elder, had a rather pretty voice, and we soon began to be treated to family concerts at which Olivier accompanied her as she sang Debussy or Fauré ... Jeanne had a bad influence on Olivier, turning him against religion. She came across a copy of Renan's *Life of Jesus* and that was that; she became deeply anti-religious, to my, and especially to my wife's, despair. Jeanne's ideas destroyed Olivier's devotion and gave rise to furious arguments within the family. But I digress. The fact is that Olivier embarked on a career as a violinist and, having graduated with distinction from the Conservatoire, at the age of twenty-five joined the Paris Symphony Orchestra under the direction of Pierre Monteux.

In the spring of 1932, the orchestra went to perform in Berlin and other German cities. Olivier came home to spend a few days in Andigny that summer. He was accompanied by a beautiful young girl, blonde with languid, laughing eyes. My son introduced her as a German actress, Elsie Berger, whom he had met at a reception thrown by the French embassy in Berlin. Olivier surprised us by announcing that they were engaged, but that Elsie – her stage name, for her real name was Ilse Wolffsohn – would soon have to return to her country, where, despite her extreme youth, she had already starred in many films. My son's ravishing conquest was only nineteen years old!

During their stay, my wife Marguerite, who was immovable on the matter (and I might add – please excuse my indiscretion – that while we still shared a room, we had had no physical relations for about a year), insisted that Ilse sleep alone in one of the guest rooms. Knowing his mother's principles, Olivier made no objection, but it became clear to me that when they went off on their long walks through the countryside, boating excursions on the Seine, or to visit our local castle, their relations were no longer chaste. The way they smiled at each other, touched or exchanged tender, intimate glances at the least opportunity told the whole story. On several occasions at night, I heard furtive footsteps in the hallway, stifled laughter, doors discreetly opened and closed. Marguerite pretended to notice none of it. And Jeanne, who joined us at weekends, immediately adopted the young German as her little sister. As for me ...

I am trying to recollect the confusion of my feelings in those early days. Like Olivier, and then Jeanne, I was undoubtedly smitten. The

German girl had – and still has, though to a lesser extent than then – a very particular way of putting one instantly at ease, a warm eloquence, a disarming enthusiasm, and a candour that was tempered by her remarkable delicacy and sensitivity. On her very first night with us, our guest sat at the piano and played us Schubert's lieder and a few Bach partitas. My gaze was constantly drawn to her shoulders, visible beneath her diaphanous dress, and the golden hair gathered at the nape of her neck.

The young actress had received the very best education in Berlin. She spoke several languages and had even read – in translation, sadly – my best collection of poems, *Ode to Nemesis,* and, in the original, two of my best-known 'war' novels, *The Skirmish* and *The Ordeal* (if memory serves; and I won't pretend that I wasn't flattered). The latter is the book in which I recount, through the epic battlefield experience of Captain Dandigny, how I lost my left forearm on 16 October 1918 while liberating Acy, near Rethel, when Gouraud's army foiled the German counterattack (but we've discussed all this already at our chess games). I hastened to offer Ilse the French edition, dedicated to her, of *Ode to Nemesis*, and we had several opportunities for intimate discussions of poetry, philosophy, literature or History – meandering conversations in which I was impressed by such extensive learning in one so young and apparently so innocent, who soon abandoned the respectful, conventional 'Monsieur' for the more casual 'Paul-Jean' – and that, too, was a source of pleasure to me. Despite our vast difference in age, I soon felt us becoming the best friends in the world. When Jeanne and I (for Marguerite, I recall, had all of a sudden decided to stay at home and had violently slammed the garden gate behind us) accompanied the couple to Andigny station, I expressed the hope that the actress's return to the capital, and then on to Germany where a new production awaited her, would not be a lasting one, and that my son's choice – one of the first of which, to my surprise, I entirely approved

– would soon be cemented in a union that would offer my later years the delicious presence and ever-fresh vision of that most charming and intelligent of nymphs.

That she was German bothered me not in the least, even if I had once fought against her people – your own, Monsieur le Commandant. But remember those early years of the 1930s; Europe had been transformed. Between 1918 and 1930 three empires – the Russian, the German and the Austrian – had been wiped off the map, and eight young States had been born, new hues among the expanded, shrunken or reshaped splashes of colour representing the various powers. Alongside ancient wounds, some only partially healed, the treaties had opened fresh ones. How long could it all hold together? Would the disintegration of that fragile edifice cost Europe another four years of war, hundreds of thousands of homes destroyed, billions upon billions spent, more than ten million killed and thirty million maimed, widowed and orphaned?

The policies of England and France to monopolise trade with their colonies represented a serious threat to Germany and Italy. As for the peace treaties, they had in no way enriched Italy, which was poor, and had seriously impoverished Germany, which was rich. If things continued this way, it seemed to me that a new war was inevitable, and sooner rather than later.

England, not Germany, is the age-old enemy of France, as Dunkirk and Mers-el-Kébir have proved yet again. I saw a Franco-German rapprochement as the only chance for a lasting European peace. The journalist Gustave Hervé, an ardent admirer of Hitler even before he became Reich Chancellor, suggested to the leaders of the Nazi Party that the Treaty of Versailles ought to be revised, to which your paper the *Völkischer Beobachter* responded favourably. In the introduction to his book *Une Voix de France*, translated and published in your country, Hervé wrote: 'The National Socialist moment cannot come too soon to France, and when it does it will ring in the hour of Franco-German reconciliation.'

Finding such ideas convincing, I signed up as an active member of the Parti Socialiste National founded by Gustave Hervé in 1929 around his newspaper *La Victoire*.

In July 1932, the military coup that set the stage for the rise of your Führer took place in Berlin.

That autumn, preceded by its steamy reputation, a film featuring Elsie Berger came to our screens. It was the notorious *Mädchen in Uniform*, the work of film-maker Leontine Sagan; shot a year earlier, it had enjoyed great success in your country and then had the honour of being chosen to represent Germany abroad. It was banned a few years later by the government of Chancellor Hitler – more for its critique of authority, perhaps, than for its sapphic content.

Under some pretext or other, I drove myself to Paris to attend a screening at a picture house on the Champs-Élysées. If you have seen these 'young girls in uniform', Monsieur le Commandant, you will no doubt remember the storyline. I myself remember it as if it were only yesterday that I had seen the all-female production. Orphaned at fourteen, Manuela, played by Hertha Thiele, is enrolled at a boarding school run with an iron fist by the sour Fraülein von Nordeck. Although she is welcomed by her classmates, the newcomer keeps herself to herself at first, until she projects her need for affection onto her literature teacher, Fraülein von Bernburg (played by Dorothea Wieck), the only adult who is sensitive to the feelings of the young boarders. The ardent friendship that the orphan feels for her elder becomes deeper, restoring her *joie de vivre*. Following her triumph in a staging of *Don Carlos*, in which she plays the lead role dressed as a man, she gets drunk and confesses her love for her literature teacher to her dumbfounded classmates.

While I appreciated the originality of the story and the talent of the actors, I had eyes only for Elsie Berger, in her all-too-brief appearances as the heroine's best friend. My son's fiancée glowed on screen with a charm comparable to that of her peers Miriam Hopkins, Nancy Carroll or Leila Hyams – three pretty blondes appearing in the pictures of that time, and whom the German resembled. But Ilse's voice and mannerisms were all her own. And to this very day, her almost silent expression of jealous admiration for her best friend's bold confession seems to me to epitomise the eternal temptation of adventure and flight, perdition even, that spirit of adolescence and rebellion that society requires us to set aside, or to extirpate. Yet it seems to me that this spirit of adventure – which is in fact a thirst for creation, for God's work – is not a bad thing in itself.

And it occurred to me that Ilse, too, barely out of adolescence herself when I had met her that summer, had yet to find a way to harness the ambition, the impetuous drive, the desire to experiment, to learn and to embrace things, that was bubbling inside her – that noble, grandiose self-belief whose rightful use it is our task to discover. And, truth be told, I doubted that Olivier was man enough to respond to such yearning.

3.

For several long months we heard no more about Ilse Wolffsohn. All through the autumn, and then the winter, I was taken up with calling upon members of the Académie Française, and inviting some of their number to dine at la Tour d'Argent, Prunier or Lapérouse. This was the third time I had set my sights on a seat in the Institute. I won't go into the old grudges and jealousies that had scuttled my two previous attempts, the latter of which had been particularly painful to me. The elections in the spring represented my last chance. I beat my rival by a single vote in the second ballot and was enrolled in the immortal assembly, taking a seat that had once been occupied by the Dreyfusard Sully Prudhomme. As you might imagine, I would have preferred to take Racine's seat! François Mauriac, who was younger than I, was elected a few months later; I would have found it humiliating had it happened the other way round.

The year 1933 was equally important to your country, Monsieur le Commandant, as Adolf Hitler rose to the chancellorship in January and Germany withdrew from the League of Nations just a few months later, the first step in a plan to liberate herself from all encumbrances in order to achieve her great destiny.

In November, *Le Matin* and *L'Information*, our most influential financial newspaper, printed interviews with Chancellor Hitler, conducted by Monsieur de Brinon, in which the great man guaranteed French security and expressed the finest regard for our country.

Ilse Wolffsohn returned to France at Christmas that year, spending the holidays with us in Andigny. I went to meet the young actress and my son at the station, accompanied by Marguerite. To me, Ilse's complexion seemed waxen, her face thinner. Olivier mentioned that she was still recovering from a nasty bout of flu, and that she had family worries. I must admit that my wife and I knew next to nothing about the Wolffsohns. Ilse, whose parents Olivier had met but once in Berlin, rarely mentioned them, and neither did my son. All we were able to gather was that her father was a chemist working in heavy industry, and that she had a younger brother, a student.

When the children married in March 1934, it was that young man, Franz, who travelled from Germany for the ceremony, which was held in l'Église de la Madeleine. No other member of the family was present. It was a beautiful, big wedding; many members of the Academy did me the honour of attending. Ilse, delicate and radiant in her white veil, looked like a young goddess descended from the Nordic pantheon, and all without exception were love-struck. The student brother, a pleasant-looking but serious young man, shook me firmly by the hand and murmured solemnly in impeccable French: 'Monsieur Husson, I am entrusting Dorte to you. So that through you – a war hero, a member of the Academy, and a great poet – and through all you represent, the spirit of Eternal France may watch over her!' He called his sister 'Dorte', no doubt an affectionate nickname she had had since childhood. I did not have the opportunity to talk to him again. Early the next day, Franz Wolffsohn boarded a train at the Gare de l'Est and we never saw him again.

I feel I should mention here that last year, on the occasion of the French writers' visit to Berlin, I was saddened to learn that the young man, a member of a subversive organisation hostile to the government of the Third Reich, had been arrested, condemned to death and executed in 1940 at Hamburg prison. It will be easy for you to verify that information. Naturally, I did not tell Ilse this; better for her to imagine him still alive and hiding somewhere in Germany.

*

The year 1934 was, dare I say, the most wonderful year of my life. At the age of fifty-eight, in full possession of my intellectual and physical powers, I felt my literary efforts reaching their zenith. My work had been translated into any number of languages and performed in the best theatres; each of my novels had been hailed as a masterpiece by the critics. In the autumn, I was awarded the Prix Renaudot. My poetry collections were studied in schools and academies. I was offered very well-remunerated lectures. Unlike that of so many others, my wealth had barely been touched by the economic chaos, thanks to some wise investments and to two buildings in Paris that had come with Marguerite's dowry. My son, a gifted musician, had recently wed a splendid young actress – I hoped that my daughter Jeanne would soon find her way to the altar – and shortly thereafter, proud and abashed, Olivier announced that his wife was expecting a happy event in November.

Ilse seemed to have renounced her film career for good, which amazed me, since I had been so impressed by her performance in *Mädchen in Uniform*. But like Olivier I had no desire to see her head east again, and I hastened to suggest that my daughter-in-law move into Villa Némésis, far from the miasmas of the big city, at least for the duration of her pregnancy, which she could bring to term in conditions optimal for both mother and child. The idea of practising, like Victor Hugo, the 'art of being a grandfather' – which I would once have found repugnant – now enchanted me. Even Marguerite seemed to have overcome her early reservations about the German.

We gave the couple our best guest room on the third floor, with a magnificent view of the bend in the Seine, with the island and the plain beyond, all the way to the cliffs of La Roquette. My son divided his time between the Eure and the capital, where he rehearsed with the orchestra while his wife settled in as our permanent guest in Andigny.

*

My God, what memories of that fine summer!

Towards the end of June, we rented the Chalet Haset in Trouville – a little gem of art nouveau architecture – for ten days. The races and the Grand Prix de Paris were over and the season was just beginning; crowds invaded the boardwalk and pier, and all who were considered, in Paris and abroad, to be major figures in the arts, the nobility, finance and politics seemed to have come together to mount a common, elegant assault on the Normandy coast, jostling and mingling and swept up in the same whirlwind of activity. The recent troubles – the night of 6 February, 'the magnificent, instinctive revolt, the night of sacrifice', as it was welcomed by Robert Brasillach, that had rattled the Whore Republic, and the Bolshevik protests six days later – seemed to have been forgotten, at least for the duration of the summer season. Lounging serenely on the soft sand of the beach at the end of the day, I fell victim to a fantasy as I watched Ilse in the orange light of sunset, my eyes following her as she strolled along the water's edge on my wife's arm, the waves arriving and dying at their feet, their dresses blowing as one in the breeze. I fancied that I had suddenly been restored to my youth in the Belle Époque …

I noticed, too, that the young woman was filling out at the waist. That face whose charming profile I so admired, now aglow in the failing light, radiated the promise of the new life growing within her. The only sorrow I felt, for a brief instant – the confession pains me, but you will read others far more terrible by the end of this letter – was the bitter, jealous regret of not being myself the source of that tiny seed now germinating in those tender depths.

In November of that year 1934, the Franco-German Committee was established under the auspices of your current Ambassador to Paris, His Excellency Monsieur Otto Abetz. The members of the French

Guidance Committee were:

Monsieur Fernand de Brinon, now Ambassador of the Vichy Government to Paris;

Monsieur Georges Scapini, Deputy, now Envoy for prisoners of war;

Monsieur Gaston Henry-Haye, Senator, now Ambassador of France to Washington, DC;

Monsieur Gaston Bergery, Deputy, now Ambassador to Ankara;

Monsieur François Piétri, Deputy, now Ambassador to Madrid;

Monsieur Jean Montigny, Deputy, former colleague of Monsieur Laval;

Monsieur Jean Goy, Deputy, President of the Union Nationale des Combattants and ardent follower of the Maréchal since 1935;

Professor Fourneau of the Academy of Medicine;

My friend and colleague Abel Bonnard of the Académie Française, now Minister of National Education;

Professor Bernard Faÿ, current Director of the Bibliothèque Nationale;

and me, Paul-Jean Husson.

My granddaughter Hermione was born on 2 October 1934, six weeks before her due date. The newborn being healthy and of normal weight, I concluded that she had actually been conceived several weeks before the wedding. Such things are of little importance to me. My wife, on the other hand, sought to keep up appearances by referring to Hermione for months as our 'adorable little premature baby'.

What did bother me, however, was that I had been expecting to welcome a miniature Ilse into the bosom of my family – a darling little blonde with her mother's laughing blue eyes – whereas our Hermione had an olive complexion, brown eyes and dark hair. Just like my son Olivier, that is.

Is that why I almost never behaved like the doting and protective grandfather that I should so have loved to be? The baby and later the toddler would laugh as she held out her little arms to me, but I could only ever respond with reticence to her touching invitations. I was wary when I picked Hermione up, hugged her reluctantly and hastened to find someone to relieve me of her. I now ask myself: Was it because she looked too much like Olivier, the son who was so different from me and over whom I continued to prefer my darling Jeanne?

Or was it because I was already beginning to suspect *something else*?

4.

The years passed.

Beyond the Rhine, your Reich created its first three Panzer divisions. In 1935, Marshal Göring – who had met Maréchal Pétain and Pierre Laval (then Minister of Foreign Affairs and soon to become President of the Council) in Warsaw on the occasion of the funeral of Marshal Pilsudski, and found them to be congenial – announced that his country was in the process of creating a powerful air force to include, in addition to numerous fighters, a significant number of bombers and a strong assault command.

The League of Nations could offer nothing more than token protests to these treaty violations. The French Nation, gangrenous with the corrupting individualism born of that absurd republican theory of human rights, seemed to be mired in staggering apathy. Democratic anarchy, so lucidly denounced by Charles Maurras, had unleashed the four scourges upon us: Jewish, Protestant, Foreigner and Freemason. Disorder was paving the way for the downfall of the Motherland, and I could not fail to register the irreversible debasement of France that had long cost us our rightful place in the world – *first* place.

All this time, our little Hermione was growing. Tawny, joyful, intelligent. The only faults I found in her were suggestions of frivolity and pridefulness, which are readily forgivable in a child.

Ilse, barely touched by maternity, was as young, radiant and beautiful as ever, the light that, on each of her visits to Normandy, illuminated my existence.

Olivier became First Violin of the Paris Symphony Orchestra.

My son began, with my approval, to enquire into obtaining French nationality for Ilse on the basis of new laws authorising it after one year of marriage to a French citizen and residence on national territory.

I wrote and wrote, showered with meaningless honours as the Whore Republic wallowed in her filth. The year 1936 brought my ancient Gallo-Roman nation the humiliation of being governed by a Jew, Léon Blum – as cunning as a Talmudic scholar, as perfidious as a scorpion, as grudging as a eunuch and as hate-filled as a viper – a Bulgarian, German, Jewish cross-breed, a prophet of error, a glum-faced Machiavelli grafted onto the head of France. In Paris, radio took on a Yiddish accent. Drawn from the darkest ghettos of the Orient by the news of their racial triumph, the hook-noses and crinkle-hairs were suddenly everywhere. Ashkenazis fleeing the ghettos of Poland and Romania flooded in by the hundred thousand. Members of this rabble succeeded in having themselves stripped of their national rights in order to be shielded from expulsion, while their precarious health landed them in our hospitals in their thousands. And so they came – the misfits, the bloodsuckers, the crippled. France had become the world's cesspool. Our access roads became sewers, turning our lands into a swamp that grew more swarming and fetid by the day. It was a vast tide of Neapolitan scum, Levantine dregs, dismal Slavic stench, appalling Andalusian destitution, the spawn of Abraham and Judean pitch.

Under the banner of the right to asylum, political refugees and common-law criminals were allowed in helter-skelter and without the slightest hindrance. All agreed on one point at least: their right to treat us as a conquered country. While some stole the bread out of French workers' mouths, others continuously insulted our patriotism, and did it, what's more, in our own newspapers. It was our duty to react. My friends and I took up our pens to demand the immediate closure of our borders. As my colleague Giraudoux, soon to be named commissioner in the Ministry of Information, declared without ambiguity, we were 'in full agreement with Hitler that politics rises to its highest nature only when it is racial'.[3] Gustave Hervé brought out a revised second edition of his book *C'est Pétain qu'il nous faut*, its cover adorned with a portrait of the Maréchal (then Vice-President of the High War Council). The printing was overseen by Paul Ferdonnet, who would later be French-language programmer for your Radio Stuttgart.

I saw the red flags – rags drenched in the blood of the innocent victims of successive revolutions – flying over the silkworks and glass factory of Andigny, now occupied by workers tricked and led astray by Moscow's union activists and agents. In Spain, Bolshevism and anarchy stood in the way of the righteous independence advocated by General Franco and the Church. My colleague Georges Bernanos, although a Christian, failed to understand the basic nature of the struggle, and we fell out. Happily, most of my colleagues in letters and ideas remained firmly on my side. The Académie Française, by the pens of eleven of its members, including me, had supported the action of the Italian Champions of Civilisation against the savage Ethiopians of Abyssinia. Maurras was elected to join us in the elite, where he naturally enjoyed my support. None of us hesitated to make our voices heard in the newspapers and weekly publications, where we expressed with righteous indignation what the vast majority of Frenchmen believed but kept to themselves: that the Jews were stealing work from our fellow citizens, illegally invading the country, and preparing for the 'Jewish revolution' in which Léon Blum was complicit. They would soon conspire to drag France, which was militarily unprepared, into their war of revenge and plunge us all into the abyss!

In 1937, Stalin's henchmen exploded bombs in the heart of Paris, in two buildings belonging to the employers' council. Minister Dormoy and a few hacks in the pay of the Soviets attributed the attacks to a secret society known as 'the Cowl' in preparation for a coup that supposedly enjoyed support in the Army. Arrests were made even within the Maréchal's inner circle, but it was all lies, shameless lies. Calumny spread by vermin!

But let us move on, Monsieur le Commandant. The time has come for me to … My hand rebels against broaching the tale of the first of the terrible tragedies that struck us to the core.

It was summer, late summer, 1938. Europe, you will recall, was awash with rumours of war. Hermione would soon turn four. My son was on tour in Scotland with his orchestra. Ilse and her daughter were spending the season with us. My daughter Jeanne – who had recently introduced us to her fiancé, a graduate of the École Normale Supérieure whose ideas were at odds with my own – was supposed to stay with us for a few days, by herself, and then join this boy in the South of France to meet his family before he was called up (all young men were expecting to be dispatched post-haste to the trenches).

Whose idea was it to go for a boat ride that sunny afternoon? Certainly not mine; perhaps it was Jeanne's, or Ilse's. Both of them rose from their deckchairs and took the little one with them, with the intention of 'doing a once-round-the-island'. I wasn't especially concerned; the weather was fine, there was hardly a breath of wind, and my daughter and daughter-in-law were both excellent swimmers. Only Marguerite protested, in vain. My wife and I watched as the three of them went laughing through the garden gate, crossed Quai de Verdun and descended to the jetty where we docked our little boat in the summer.

Half an hour later, I heard cries, and then the entrance bell jangling furiously. I saw Ilse ringing at the garden gate. Terrified, drenched to the skin and carrying little Hermione, who was also soaking and howling in her mother's arms.

I ran down to the waterside. Our boat had slipped its ropes and was being carried away on the river current. Empty. I jumped into the water, but my artificial arm, heavy and useless, prevented me from getting very far. How I cursed that German mortar that day! I called out to some sailors, who came running, diving from their boats or the end of the jetty. Following Ilse's directions from the embankment, where she pointed towards the site of the accident, these good men did their best … But the dark waters and the powerful current held on to their prey, invisible and lost. We searched until twilight before returning to land, death in our souls.

My daughter-in-law explained what had happened. The wake from an enormous empty barge tearing along the Seine had rocked the skiff, giving little Hermione a sudden fright. The child had scurried to the side, and Ilse, afraid she would tumble overboard, had leapt forward to grab her. As a result, the boat had rolled again, more violently this time. Ilse, carried by the momentum, had fallen into the water with the child. Jeanne had immediately dived to their assistance.

Having saved her child, Ilse had pulled herself back on board with great difficulty, only to find no trace of my daughter. There was no sign of her in the water, either.

Had Jeanne been hit on the head by one of the oars? Or struck the bottom of the boat as she rose from her dive? Or was she the victim of cramp or hypothermia? We never knew. Forty-eight hours later, a body was found at Saint-Pierre-du-Vauvray lock and brought to town. I went to the police station alone to identify it. My Jeanne was just a horrible thing, swollen and greenish, that I recognised from her bathing costume.

Dr Dimey had been called to the house to give sedative injections to my wife and Ilse, both of whom were in shock. The doctor's wife took Hermione home with her for a while.

I refused all medication, retreating into silence.

I tried to meditate on Malherbe's consolation:

> To want what God wants
> Is the only study
> That can give us peace.

The burial took place at Andigny cemetery, in the family vault. Marguerite did not have the strength to attend. And in any case, I preferred it that way. The Academy sent several members, among them the two Abels — my friends Hermant and Bonnard. The fiancé arrived from the provinces accompanied by an uncle. They offered their awkward condolences. At least my Jeanne will never belong to that nonentity, I thought, and was immediately stricken with nausea at the idea that I had been reduced to grasping at such straws in order to stave off despair. Olivier, alerted by telegram in Scotland, was with us by then, supporting his wife, whose pale and haggard face was frightening to behold.

The next day, which also marked the return of Daladier and Chamberlain from Munich, we went to retrieve Hermione, the innocent cause of my daughter's death, and I found that I could not bear to be near her.

And yet, I found it impossible to blame Ilse.

5.

Alone with my wife, I stayed at the villa on the banks of the river that had taken Jeanne.

Olivier, the German and the little one did not join us either for Christmas or for New Year, preferring to spend the holidays in Megève.

Marguerite appeared to have put her depression behind her. At least, in the eyes of those who did not know her very well. Towards the end of winter, she returned the manuscript of my latest novel – I made her read everything I wrote before sending it to my publisher – with a comment that escapes me for the moment, but which struck me as odd at the time. A somewhat peculiar sentence that troubled me. I let it pass. But then, a few weeks later, my wife began with increasing frequency to struggle to find her words. One might perhaps have put it down to her age, which I did to start with, but the symptom began to occur more and more frequently. I noticed, too, that she was favouring her left leg, moving heavily and painfully, and that she complained of the weight of her basket on market days. I decided that the cook should go in her stead, but when Marguerite dictated the shopping list, she could no longer find such commonplace words as 'potatoes' or 'cheese'.

Dr Dimey was called in for a consultation, and diagnosed an acute form of melancholy brought on by the shock of Jeanne's death. He prescribed herbal remedies and vitamins, and suggested a cure in Divonne, where the waters were reputed to be excellent for neurasthenia.

One morning, before I had even had a chance to buy our train tickets or book a hotel room, Marguerite was unable to rise from our bed without my assistance. Dismayed and fearing meningitis – for she had been feverish and vomiting the night before – I drove her at once to Paris in our old Rochet-Schneider to see a famous nerve specialist whom my cousin Henri had recommended. Following a lengthy examination of his patient, Professor Jacob beckoned me into the neighbouring room, his face a picture of solemn concern. He feared a brain tumour, and recommended immediate hospitalisation in his ward at Salpêtrière, where he could do more thorough testing with a view towards possible surgery.

I chose for the moment not to inform Olivier or to move in with him on Rue Richer; instead, I took a room in a hotel by the Gare d'Austerlitz in order to be near my wife and visit her every day. I had a meeting with the professor a week later in his consulting room at the hospital. The Jew, all puffed up with his scientific wisdom, announced bluntly that there was indeed a brain tumour, and that it had already grown to such an extent that it was inoperable, even with the widest possible trephination. Crushed, I asked him how my wife's condition would develop.

'Injections will temporarily reduce the inflammation,' Jacob explained with a serenity that I found unbearable, 'so you can expect a mild improvement for the next three or four weeks. Then your wife's mental and physical health will gradually weaken as the tumour grows. I advise you to have Madame Husson hospitalised near your home. She is in no pain. You can keep the gravity of her condition from her until the very end.'

I asked in a subdued voice when that end might come. The Yid shrugged his shoulders and sighed.

'There is no way to predict that, my dear Monsieur. It could be anywhere between four and nine months …'

An ambulance took Marguerite home to Andigny, while I followed in the car. I will spare you, Monsieur le Commandant, a description of my feelings on that funereal journey. My wife was found a room in the Saint-Jacques hospice only a few paces from our house, and enjoyed a practically identical view of the Seine.

I visited Marguerite there every day. The first month, as the hook-nosed specialist had predicted, she seemed to return to normal, and I allowed myself to hope once again. Perhaps the tumour would vanish as it had appeared, mysteriously and in silence? Perhaps the injections and the medicine were enough to stop it, shrink it, eradicate it? I told my wife that she was suffering from a nervous ailment that was better treated here than at home. She seemed to be satisfied with the explanation. Olivier, Ilse and the child came to see us every weekend. We took tea and pastries in the sickroom, which we filled with chatter. Marguerite would fall into a doze, sinking into a vague torpor that I attributed to inactivity or the drugs. We hugged her and tiptoed from the room. The others pretended to share my optimism when I accompanied them to the railway station. On the way there, I noticed the first signs of spring, the budding trees. I took these signs to indicate that Our Lord, in thus demonstrating his eternal power, would come to our assistance. 'Help yourself, and Heaven will help you.' Yes indeed, we had to hold fast, as we did at Verdun! The illness, and the prognosis delivered by the sinister Jew of Salpêtrière, would be overthrown!

One Sunday in early April as I joined my family in the sickroom, I witnessed an unusual spectacle. Marguerite was holding Hermione and teaching her what I took at first to be a new game. The girl was told to rub her nose with the index finger of each hand in turn, drawing the skin upwards towards her brow, while my wife sang a little ditty, smiling and saying over and over, 'My nose is growing straight, my nose is growing straight, pretty little nose so nice and straight ...' My son was absent, but Ilse was livid, watching the performance in silence. The tension in the room was palpable. Upon catching sight of me, my daughter-in-law threw me a furtive glance before grabbing the child forcefully from her grandmother. I forgot the incident as we chatted about one thing or another. Marguerite, her eyes wandering, soon lost interest in Hermione as she followed, or rather pretended to follow, the conversation.

On my solitary walk back to the villa from the station, I found myself humming a tune, and realised that Marguerite's childish and catchy song had stuck in my head. 'Pretty little nose so nice and straight ...' I stopped in my tracks, suddenly understanding what it was that my wife, without ever having mentioned it, had seen. Or believed she had seen.

And it struck me that this thought, this vague and nebulous suspicion, had been nagging at me for months without my having been consciously aware of it.

Yet I could hardly confront my daughter-in-law point-blank with the question. What about Olivier? He was sensitive and might well take it amiss. As things stood, our relations were already embittered enough. I decided to wait for an opportune moment to bring it up casually. That in itself would be no simple task, as my son continued to object to my articles in the French press, although they merely addressed the self-evident truth that in every country where the children of Abraham decide to proliferate they pose a significant national and social threat. But as I generally sought to avoid family quarrels, I chose to put the matter off to another time.

The following month, on a sudden whim I bought a First Empire painting that I had seen in the window of the Galerie Charpentier. The canvas belonged to some wealthy Parisian Jews who were selling their collection before emigrating to America. The dealer sold it to me at a reasonable price, while still ensuring a handsome profit for himself, since the Yids were in a hurry. The painting, by Louis-Léopold Boilly, was entitled *Amour familial*. In a corner of a bourgeois drawing room, a lovely young brown-haired woman is sitting on a sofa, dressed in an ample silk negligee. Even as she embraces her three children, her face in profile, she places a tender kiss on the cheek of her husband, who, one arm draped across the back of the sofa, leans in turn across the tight little ensemble to kiss the forehead of his eldest daughter. The latter raises her eyes to her father, while the two little ones hug one another as they cling to their mother's bosom.

This edifying and touching image of a close-knit family, reminiscent of the allegorical work of Greuze some decades earlier, unsettled me for I recognised in it the protagonists of a true story, or one that might have been. The man was me in my younger days. The woman bore a striking resemblance to Marguerite as a young mother. The eldest child was Jeanne; the son, in the middle, was Olivier at six or seven. And the exquisite youngest one, with her blue eyes, anxious expression, round cheeks, porcelain complexion and blonde hair, being affectionately kissed on the ear by her brother – wasn't she the very picture of Ilse? The relative ages matched in any case. I chose to decide that the painting did indeed portray my daughter-in-law, that ravishing poppet from beyond the Rhine whom our Christian family had adopted.

I paid the dealer, took the painting home to Andigny, and had it hung forthwith in the drawing room.

In May, the season of flowers and communions, a processional of girl communicants heading towards our cathedral rekindled an inchoate anxiety in my heart. The children of our city, draped in guileless probity and immaculate veils, were on their way to bring their reverent dreams to fruition beneath the splendours of the stained glass. I followed the processional in a fog. I entered the cathedral, greeting a few acquaintances, neighbours and tradesmen. At the centre of the nave, decorated for this holy day, the communicants gathered like a troupe of white angels – some of whom, the prettiest, resembled Ilse on her wedding day – enveloped in the symbolic purity of lilies. They held hands in solemn silence, little brides of the faith trembling with sacred anticipation as they awaited the mystical moment of divine revelation. One girl, overcome with emotion, dropped her candle, knocking down the one in front, which set off a chain reaction like a game of skittles. Murmurs of disapproval rose from the pews. The girl who had started it all fainted and was carried off. Calm was restored in the church, and I fell to thinking.

In a few years it would be our Hermione's turn to join the May processional in white. Her brown hair haloed by the insubstantial veil, she would be full of devotion reciting her catechism, a book of canticles on her knees, as she prepared to be brushed by the wings of a great happiness. But as I sat and watched among the murmuring crowd in the ancient cathedral, I was thinking: *Is my granddaughter fully entitled to receive that divine and sacred communion? Is she truly a member of the flock of God's children?*

6.

I could no longer bear to remain in such a state of uncertainty. On the occasion of a weekly meeting of the Academy, I put in a request at the Institute for the address of a service specialising in private investigations. Our secretary provided me with the requisite information, and I proceeded to the office, which was located, rather poetically, on Rue de la Lune in the second arrondissement, next door to the School of Wireless Telegraphy. I explained to the man who received me that I was seeking any available information about a Monsieur and Madame Wolffsohn of Berlin, whose daughter had been an actress in the early thirties. The investigator replied that such an inquiry would be very costly, as an assistant would have to be sent to Germany for several weeks, and in these troubled times. I insisted that expense was no object, adding that what I most wanted to know was whether these people might by chance be Jews. The man gave me a knowing look, as if to say that my request was more common than I had thought. He promised me results within two months at the latest, and asked for a rather sizeable advance that I paid without haggling.

That night I had dinner with Louis-Charles Royer, the gifted author of *La Maîtresse noire*. Maurice Dekobra was there too. Like Geneviève Tabouis, who had so accurately predicted the latest crises, he believed that war was now inevitable. Having spent the night at the flat of Olivier and Ilse – whom I no longer dared to look in the eye – I returned to Andigny, where I was alarmed by a change in Marguerite's demeanour. She would fly into a temper at the least provocation, raging, her gaze fixed and hard and lit by a spark of madness, demanding information on a subject that, once again groping for the right word, she was unable to explain to me.

This interlude of abrupt and frequent tantrums lasted barely a month. As summer approached my wife grew slowly but irremediably weaker. I was the disconsolate and powerless witness to this irreversible deterioration. Marguerite spoke less and less, her conversation for the most part without sense. Ilse threw me long, sorrowful looks. Olivier rarely visited. The harvest came three weeks late because an early frost the previous autumn had compelled our farmers to re-sow a third of their fields. On 4 July, I was invited to the wedding of my old friend (and new member of the Académie Goncourt) Sacha Guitry at the church of Fontenay-le-Fleury, in the parish of the Château de Ternay, which he had recently bought.

The great throng of notables included Monseigneur Merio, Bishop of Versailles, who sanctified the union between Sacha and young Geneviève; Prince Poniatowski; Monsieur André Magre, Secretary General of the Presidency of the Republic; Prefect of Police Langeron; Monsieur Huisman, the Jewish Director of the Beaux-Arts; Goncourt academician René Benjamin; Maurice Martin du Gard, Max Maurey, Lisette Lanvin, the humorist Tristan Bernard (another Jew, but very witty) … Our dear host took us on a tour of Napoleon's room, which he had reconstructed most faithfully. This wonderful, worldly day in the country was a welcome break from the monotony of the bedside and the nauseating miasmas of the sickroom, and the sole happy interlude from the nightmare that held me in its grip.

Upon my return, the maid informed me of a telephone call received in my absence from an agency in Paris. I called back immediately. It was from the detective agency – their man was back from Berlin, and a confidential report awaited me at Rue de la Lune.

I reproduce that report for you here, Monsieur le Commandant:

DARDANNE AGENCY
14 Rue de la Lune, Paris 2e
Investigations, surveillance.
Discretion guaranteed.

File: <u>WOLFFSOHN/BERGER</u>

Client:
Monsieur P.-J. Husson
20 Quai de Verdun
Andigny, Département de l'Eure

FIRST REPORT

Thomas WOLFFSOHN, born 8 January 1882 in Berlin, Germany.

Marta LEESER, wife of WOLFFSOHN, born 29 June 1887 in Frankfurt, Germany.

Domicile (until November 1938): 32 Lützowstrasse, Berlin W 35.

Children: Ilse Maria Dorothea, born 3 April 1913 in Berlin, and Franz Emil, born 24 October 1915 in Berlin.

Profession of Thomas WOLFFSOHN: Chemical engineer. Former employer: I.G. Farben company. Dismissed in March 1938.

Religion: Jewish. The WOLFFSOHNs are an Israelite family originally from Hamburg but for the past six generations resident in Berlin, where they are members of German high society; the LEESERs are Jews from the Palatinate; Thomas WOLFFSOHN is a distant relative of Rabbi Chacham Tzvi ASHKENAZI, who came to Hamburg in 1690, where he founded a Talmudic school before being appointed rabbi of Amsterdam.

Current address: unknown. Monsieur and Madame

WOLFFSOHN reserved two berths for Palestine at the Berlin branch of Palestine & Orient Lloyd on 6 November 1938 (shortly before the nationwide pogrom of 9 November). Their names were not found on the list of embarked passengers. The house at 32 Lützowstrasse has been stripped of its furnishings, and most of its windows have been smashed.

Ilse WOLFFSOHN (under the stage name Elsie BERGER) began her acting career with a small role in *Spies* (director: Fritz LANG) and has featured in a number of German and Austrian films since 1927, including *Das Lied ist aus* (director: Géza VON BOLVÁRY), *Das Flötenkonzert von Sans-souci* (director: Gustav UCICKY), *Mädchen in Uniform* (director: Leontine SAGAN), *Der Kongress tanzt* (director: Erik CHARELL), and *Anna und Elisabeth* (director: Frank WISBAR). Miss BERGER had to abandon her career because of her religion. It would appear that she no longer lives in Germany.

Franz WOLFFSOHN disappeared two years ago and is named in a file of individuals sought by the German police for terrorist activities. He is accused of having served as liaison to Czech patriots plotting the assassination of Chancellor HITLER on 1 April, on the occasion of the launching of the *Tirpitz*.

Having hurried over to the Dardanne Agency, I pored over the report and the additional notes which I have retained and which are at your disposal. I thanked the investigator and settled the account. The man offered to pursue the inquiry – for instance, by following the trail of Elsie Berger/Ilse Wolffsohn, who might have emigrated to France, England or even the United States (like many other Jewish actors and film-makers) – and to inform me of the fate of her family. Or by sending an agent to Palestine. All of which, of course, would be costly. I told him there was no need, that the information I had received would suffice.

Outside on the street, I suffered an attack of vertigo. Some concerned passers-by helped me to the terrace of a café where, after downing a glass of brandy, I was restored to physical and mental equilibrium.

However, with neither the strength to return immediately to the countryside, nor the inclination to stay with my son and daughter-in-law, I spent the night in a hotel in Faubourg Saint-Germain, dining alone at Brasserie Lipp, where I shunned conversation with my acquaintances. I was subject to a range of emotions, but that which predominated was cold rage towards Olivier.

It was apparent that my son *knew*. Had known since his visit to Ilse Wolffsohn's parents in Berlin in 1932. Seven years had passed since then, throughout which he had withheld the truth from his mother and me. In the meantime and with the utmost urgency, Olivier had made every arrangement for Ilse to become French. In order to spare her the opprobrium that was naturally due her race in Germany. I was further struck by a new, painful thought: that perhaps the actress had seen her marriage as an opportunity to make a 'new start'. What may have been a mere whim in 1932 would have later become a practical solution, motivating her return to France.

Rather than being born of love, as I had always believed, did that not make my granddaughter the offspring of self-interest?

Unable to sleep, I feverishly turned these poisonous thoughts over and over in my mind, while beneath the windows of the hotel the boulevard was loud with the roar of automobiles, the laughter and shouts of passers-by, and conversation from the lively café terraces of Flore and Les Deux Magots, which teemed with my friends and enemies alike from the world of letters.

7

Please try to understand my state of mind that night, Monsieur le Commandant. This was not a simple case of anti-Semitism on my part – a perspective that, while perfectly justified, has sometimes incited certain excesses of conduct.

But we French must recognise – as you in your country already have, drawing the appropriate conclusions therefrom – that, alongside liberalism and its consequences, alongside selfish capitalism and deadly revolutionary Marxism, *one always and forever finds the Jews among us!* We find them in every antisocial movement, where they thrive marvellously as they gnaw, stitch by stitch, at the fabric of our traditions.

The Jewish question has often been misunderstood. I do not criticise the Yids for their work ethic (which, among other things, allowed Thomas Wolffsohn to provide his children with ease and education), or for their notorious business acumen. As you know as well as I, the gravity of the situation is that the Jews pose a *national* and *social* threat to every country in which they are to be found. National, because the Jews are stateless and assimilate only superficially into the civilisation of the country that has nonetheless honoured them with its welcome. Social, because the Jewish mind is critical and subversive to the highest degree; its seditious tendencies, being in no way mitigated by patriotic loyalty, lead it to criticise the institutions of the country to which it has attached itself, sometimes undermining and even destroying them. That is why the Jew is always so ready to involve himself in Freemasonry, or in Marxist and terrorist organisations.

We French remember only too well how many of his co-religionists won themselves ministerial and executive positions in the 'Popular Front' administration of that Jew Blum, and insinuated themselves into every level of government. Jewry had already swarmed into the medical profession *en masse* and – as I am well positioned to attest – reigned supreme in journalism and the theatre.

No less pernicious is the *moral degeneracy* of the Jews, which measures up in every way to that of the Levantines, Armenians, Greeks and other dagos, be they tradesmen or traffickers.

(I would also point out that the Jews of France continue to fight their homeland from abroad – we find them precisely among the political deserters and financial émigrés aligned with the Gaullists!)

In any case, your Führer has long understood the matter perfectly, and as for us, our Government of National Revolution has finally begun to make up for lost time. But when I discovered the hidden evil at the heart of my family, it was only 1939 – that is, the days of the Whore Republic, when the Jews were knowingly shepherding us towards disaster.

At home, the disaster had already taken place, though in this case none could have predicted it. And yet, a horrible new idea gnawed at me even more tirelessly: Was not this Jewish child – or, more precisely, half-Jewish, although I have heard it said that according to its beliefs or superstitions this religion is passed down exclusively through the mother – the catalyst of our first tragedy? Had not my beloved daughter perished because of her fatal notion to take the bored child for an outing on the river? And had not the shock of that tragic death given birth in turn to the tumour that had eroded, *stitch by stitch*, my wife's mind and nervous system? Had Our Lord not sought – through this appalling chain of events, this deadly transmission accurately mirroring the invasion of His eldest daughter, France itself – to punish us for the sacrilege of having welcomed this impure creature into the bosom of our good Christian family?

Upon further reflection, however, the *true* guilty parties in this calamity, if there were any, were Olivier, and then Hermione, howsoever unwittingly. As for Ilse, she could be held responsible neither for the family in which she had chanced to be born, nor for the political circumstances that had led her to seek salvation, whether or not out of genuine love, in our eternal land of asylum, which had so often shown itself to be excessively generous.

For that matter, Monsieur Langeron, the former Prefect of Police, had explained to me, at the Guitrys' wedding luncheon, how his office undertook its practice of meticulous screening, complemented by vigilant surveillance – the threat posed by undesirables being commensurate with the difficulty of identifying them – to ensure the safety and security of all, including that of the few foreigners who were worthy of the shelter they sought in our country.

In any event, it was more than clear that my daughter-in-law had little to fear from the Prefect of Police, or from her homeland, given that even the stealthy bloodhounds of the Dardanne Agency – I smiled for the first time in hours at this thought – had been unable to track her down right there in their own town! Ilse Wolffsohn, having 'escaped' her native Germany, had become French *in full accordance with the law*. And no one had raised the least question of her religion.

The night having borne wise counsel, it was in a slightly calmer state of mind that I returned to Andigny the next day.

I had received my money's worth, that was certain. At least now I *knew*. That was enough; for the time being there was no need to go any further. My daughter-in-law was a Jew – but after all, there had to be a few good ones among them! Physically there was no way to tell. As for my granddaughter, she was half-Jewish; it may have showed in certain ways, but only if you were looking for the signs. And what of it? No one other than me and my wife – who was barely able to speak at that point – could bear witness to the truth. Ilse and Olivier, naturally, would keep their mouths shut. As to my son's in-laws, those Wolffsohns with their perhaps typical Israelite features (their racial characteristics having skipped a generation to re-emerge in Hermione), they must have emigrated to Palestine, leaving no trace of their flight. Just as well, and good riddance!

When the children returned to spend the weekend at the villa not long afterwards, I did my very best to welcome them in the most natural way, even forcing myself to play the doting grandpa with Hermione, who was rather taken aback. My daughter-in-law seemed to be grateful for that and, despite Marguerite's illness, the friendly atmosphere reminded me of the good old days, before the tragedies. On Sunday evening, I drove my family back to Paris in the car and spent the night at their flat, having been invited for the following day to the Polish embassy on Rue Saint-Dominique (now the headquarters of your German Institute), where, in that splendid old palace built for a Monegasque princess in the seventeenth century, Monsieur Lukasiewicz, the representative of the Warsaw government, held a glittering reception. Those in attendance included Paul Reynaud, the pianist Rubinstein – another Yid – and my colleague André Maurois, alias Herzog, that tiresome plagiarist whose Jewishness, in my ecumenical good humour, I was pleased to overlook. Also present were Princess Sixte de Bourbon-Parme and Princess de Faucigny-Lucinge. Although she was mobbed, Jacqueline Delubac (the former Madame Guitry), wearing a wispy dress and a white bird of paradise in her hair, graciously consented to several dances with me. I even tried to flirt, on the pretext of consoling her on her divorce and Sacha's 'treachery'.

That night in Paris, the political theatre appeared – in what can only be described as an historic irony – to favour Poland, and for the first time in that unsettled month of July the sky was clear.

War broke out six weeks later.

8

Gas masks were distributed to the people of Paris.

Olivier was mobilised and joined an armoured regiment somewhere in the East (I learned the location of his posting only after the armistice).

My daughter-in-law enrolled in a nursing course at the Union des Femmes de France.

As a commandant in the reserves, I prepared myself to be called up. In deference to my disability, I was favoured with an appointment as assistant director of the École Militaire d'Andigny, a strictly honorific post that allowed me to remain near my wife and to enjoy her few remaining months of life at her side.

The President of the Council named General Gamelin as Supreme Commander of the Franco-British armies. While I regretted that we were at war with the Germans rather than the Soviets, like all Frenchmen I was proud to place my fate in the hands of this man, whom I had seen in combat in the summer of 1918 when, as Commander of the Ninth Division, he had valiantly defended Compiègne and closed the road to Paris to your forces. He was an officer of the old school, boasting a distinguished military ascendancy, and seemed to represent all that was most pure and selfless in that profoundly national embodiment of our strength and our civilisation – the Army, which since childhood I had deemed to be one of the greatest things on Earth.

Ilse came to Andigny with Hermione in November for All Saints' Day. She had been given ten days' leave. As part of her uniform, my daughter-in-law wore a dark-blue veil and a cape of the same colour, with its white breast badge bearing a red cross and embroidered with the initials of the military first aid service. In concealing her charms, the uniform in fact multiplied them tenfold. When she removed her cape on arriving at our house, the sight of her figure elegantly outlined by her immaculate white dress was like a thunderbolt. I felt – and I have pledged to tell the full truth, Monsieur le Commandant – a wave of violent desire sweep through me. Only my sense of propriety, shame and the presence of the child restrained me from making the ill-advised gesture that, may God forgive me, I felt myself driven to commit at that moment.

That night, unable to sleep in the big bed that Marguerite no longer shared with me, I recalled the brave nurses who had cared for me following my injury, on the second floor of a castle near Toul, of which my comrades and I were cherished 'guests', and later in the military hospital at Vittel. In the ambulances at the front, or in the mobile surgical vans that picked up the wounded in the line of fire, nurses were sometimes badly injured and even killed in the crossfire. And behind the lines, how many died of overwork, or of diseases contracted while treating the contagious? Some sour souls have spoken severely of the flirtatiousness behind those white veils, but anyone with a perceptive, open mind would see that such womanly courage, preserving its devotion to grace even in the most difficult and least poetic of circumstances, was a most attractive and typically French quality – and one that Ilse had assimilated in her contact with our people. What praiseworthy endurance! How immune to revulsion, impatience and nerves they seemed to be in the face of horrendous bloodshed, pain and death!

In Paris in those terrible days – as I have already described in one of my books – at that indeterminate hour between night and dawn, one encountered women of a certain understated elegance slipping through the empty streets with short, rapid steps. Beneath the veil that covered their faces, which might be worn with the exhaustion of a vigil or taut with the effort of an early awakening, one glimpsed white hair, blonde or brown curls. Mothers, young women or girls, some were coming off the night shift after treating the wounded while others were hurrying to relieve them of their duties in the ambulances and hospitals. In the old days, they would have been coming home from the ball at that time! Their sense of having accomplished a cherished duty, or their haste to bring comfort to an injured man whom daylight was about to recall to his suffering, kept them from being defeated by their fatigue. All had a son, a husband, a brother or a fiancé over there, where the dying was going on. And each was sunk in reflection as she went; each bore silently her cross.

The image of Ilse superimposed itself upon my free-floating memories, on those veiled figures bent over the beds of pain, the faces of those angels of mercy with their tightly pulled-back hair, a mutinous lock emerging from beneath the fabric. The Elsie Berger of *Mädchen in Uniform* appeared to me, too, on the mute, flickering screen of my dreams. I saw the actress with her bright, languid eyes, her small, sensual mouth, her graceful, childlike expression as she leaned over me, whispering words of sweet comfort, pulling up the sheets and blankets, sliding her hand beneath them to stroke my shoulder, my mutilated arm, my chest heaving with emotion, then towards my lower belly. Overwhelmed, in my sleep I whispered, 'Ilse, Ilse, Ilse ...' and awoke alone in the vast moonlit room as my seed flowed.

All Saints' Day had dawned with grey cloud cover having displaced the icy, crystalline sky of the night before, and at breakfast, served by the maid in the dining room overlooking the river, a heavy silence reigned. My daughter-in-law appeared to be crushed by the rigours of her work at the hospital; the absence of Olivier, who sent her nothing but the occasional brief message from the front, screened by the military censor; and her separation from Hermione, who had been sent to live with a friend and whom she saw only rarely when she was given leave or could take holiday.

As for me, I was haunted by the memory of the previous night. In a funny way, I felt almost as if the solitary pleasure I had experienced – arising from a mere dream, to be sure, but brought on, too, by the physical presence of she with whom I was sharing breakfast, who slept under my roof, who called me by my Christian name, who bore my surname and who, for the past seven years, had shared a bed with a man born of my flesh – ultimately differed very little from that which I should have derived from actually being with her.

Over the course of my life, I have known, in the biblical sense, hundreds of women: girls of good family, peasants, servants, seamstresses, whores, countesses, romantic schoolgirls, middle-class matrons, nurses, aviatrixes, fashion models, stage actresses, loose women, students, lovelorn readers and so on. My literary fame, my rank, my medals, my disability – you can't imagine how many of these creatures were fascinated by the sight or feel of my prosthesis or my stump – seem to make me an object of singular attraction. Marguerite, who was aware of only a small fraction of my indiscretions, wisely chose to turn a blind eye and not dig too deeply.

Today, I look back over my past. What remains of those intoxicating embraces, those burning kisses, those caresses, bites, groans and cries, those follies? That wild beating of our hearts, that rising of our sap, those effusions and our divine ecstasies? What remains of them?

Nothing.

Or so little. Memories that could just as easily be illusions. Fables. Lies.

I could have made up all those liaisons I have just enumerated for you. Or you might choose not to believe me. What difference would it make? Do I even believe in them myself? I have forgotten so many names, so many faces, so many bodies …

If my past life had so little substance, I told myself as I sat at the silent table overlooking the dreary, leaf-strewn garden that lay between us and the Seine, swollen with rain and laden with broken branches … If it was so, then whether it was Ilse's own delicate, graceful hand that had brought me to a climax, or merely that of her shadow – was there really any difference?

Because it was her name, and no one else's, that I had whispered. It was she whose face and body had lifted my sword. She who had ordered my old heart to beat the attack. She who made me believe I was about to die.

That night, Elsie Berger, Ilse Husson, had been mine. Whether she was aware of it or not scarcely mattered.

The memory of that rut burned more strongly – a hundred, a thousand times more strongly – than all those flimsy recollections of love that grow confused and vanish forever into the abyss of time.

The weather outside looked cold and damp, and the breakfast dragged on. Unable to tear my mind from my nocturnal delights and the feelings they continued to elicit, I took inspiration from a reference to the fetching uniform that Ilse had worn yesterday – now replaced by a diaphanous negligee that only excited me more – to direct the conversation to those charitable young women whom I had known in Vittel in 1918.

The bourgeois ladies of the resort and those who had come for the cure – mostly the forlorn wives of officers at the front – were a constant presence at the military hospital. They were well aware that men, even those condemned to idleness, and perhaps even more so under such circumstances, have physical needs. These Frenchwomen were thus intent on consoling their fallen warriors, bedridden or hobbling on crutches, and I cited the case of one Mademoiselle de T., most likely a virgin, whose fiancé had been killed in the earliest days of the war. This rather ugly twenty-five-year-old client of the spa came regularly to the hospital, seeking out the bedsides of all without exception – even those with the most hideous facial disfigurations – and had soon earned a nickname among the patients that was so vulgar I avoided repeating it. Settled into a chair at the side of a convalescent or disabled veteran, her gaze fixed on the wall, in her sweet voice she whispered Christian words of trust and hope, while beneath the sheets her right hand …

Ilse blushed furiously, reminding me that Hermione was with us at the table. I shrugged my shoulders. What could a five-year-old understand about this tale of a hand? Her mother made a face. 'Even so …' I laughed and changed the subject.

Over the following days I devoted myself more assiduously to my granddaughter, who eventually rewarded my efforts with greater affection. Hermione had a lot of Husson in her, and of her mother, who was generally kind and happy. As to her faults, they could only come from those eastern Jews the Wolffsohns or the Leesers, and I strove to cure her of the defects of her race – pride, slothfulness, frivolity – and to nurture all that was best in her to maturity. Was I doing her a service, even supposing that I could succeed? I believed I could, and I considered the task to be a duty.

At the close of their all-too-brief visit, during the ritual goodbyes on the platform of Andigny station, I hugged Ilse – who had resumed the blue veil and long cape – holding her against me a few seconds longer than usual. My heart was beating fast; could she feel it? My little nurse extricated herself from my embrace. 'Come back soon,' I begged, turning to whisper breathlessly, 'Promise, Hermione?' The child nodded; Ilse took her by the hand and climbed onto the train without responding. I watched the red tail lights of the train recede down the tracks until they vanished into the dark night.

My son had left for the front in early September and had not yet been given leave for Paris. I calculated that my Jewish daughter-in-law had not enjoyed the carnal act in two months.

9.

It is 8.30 a.m. Unable to sleep, I rose and began to write to you before dawn, and my wrist is numb from the work. The maid has just brought me my coffee. I have asked her not to disturb me before lunch.

She is one of our sturdy peasant women from the Bocage, speaking with their typical slow drawl. Her husband works at the glassworks. Unbeknown to her, this decent woman was the inspiration for Marie-Thérèse in my *Monsieur de Saintonge*. I slept with girls of her type in my youth. I liked their candid laughter, their cheeks browned in the open air, their broad hips, their heavy, sweet-smelling breasts, their skilful hands and wrists, trained at work in our Norman dairies. I've sown quite a few bastards in the countryside; they are adults by now, most of them men, and out at work by this time of day. They rise at six, have their breakfast of soup, buttered bread and cider. In the summer, they work eleven hours in the fields without a break. My blood flows in their veins, and their sweat waters the soil.

Before I finish this letter, Monsieur le Commandant, I will have to return to the subject of these boys – or rather, one of them in particular.

God help me.

As the Maréchal explained, the French will see all their strength restored, like the giant in the fable, when their feet are once again firmly planted in the soil. For the peasant is able to live on hope:

> In the fields, nothing can be taken for granted. Work
> in itself is not enough. One must still protect the fruits

of the earth from the fickleness of the weather: frost, flood, hail, drought. The city-dweller can live from day to day. The cultivator must predict, calculate, struggle. Disappointments have no hold on such a man, who is guided by an instinct for the necessary labour and a passion for the soil. Whatever may come, he faces it, holds firm, and masters it.

France – a hardworking, thrifty and freedom-loving nation – was born of such everyday miracles. The peasant built her with his heroic patience. It is he who maintains her economic and spiritual equilibrium. The prodigious advances in our material strength have yet to tap the source of our moral strength, which is etched all the more indelibly on the heart of the peasant because he draws it from the very soil of the Homeland.[4]

The earth does not lie. It is our undying resource. It is the Homeland itself.

In giving his attention to its destiny, the Maréchal sees, in its resurgence or its decline, the very reflection of our *national* destiny.

Shortly after my little family had left, I received my first military postcard from Olivier, a scrap of blue cardboard sent from 'Postal Sector No. 165'. The printed heading read: 'This card must contain no indication of location, no description of military activity, and no name of a ranking officer.' My son wrote neither about Ilse, nor about the child, nor about his own situation; he sent trite get-well wishes to his dear little mother; spoke – God knows why – about Napoleon; and signed off with the comical 'Your sans-culotte'. At the hospice, I read the card to Marguerite, who nodded her head in silence, though I could not be certain that she understood. As the weather was fine, the ward sister allowed me to take my wife for a walk in the wheelchair, bundled up in furs over her nightgown. We strolled along the river. As we approached Quai de Verdun, I worried that the sight of our outer wall, the gables, chimneys and half-timbers of our villa – the largest and most handsome along this stretch of the Seine – might provoke some sort of crisis in Marguerite, or an overwhelming desire for home. But nothing of the sort occurred. I pushed the wheelchair slowly along to the very last pontoon, then turned round. On a Belgian barge that was passing by, a young blonde, her checked dress flapping around her bare legs, was hanging the washing out to dry. Although I was hardly able to distinguish her features at that distance, she, too, somehow reminded me of Ilse, whom I saw everywhere, here or on the streets of the capital, and whose image I was unable to shake from my thoughts.

After a political meeting with men who shared my convictions (our campaign for the return to leadership of Maréchal Pétain, who was Ambassador to Madrid at that time, was in full swing), and a reception at Academy headquarters in late November, I invited Jacqueline Delubac to dinner at the Ritz. I craved, body and soul, the distraction of a woman of quality, as I felt that I would go out of my mind if I allowed my obsession to torment me a moment longer. The maître d'hôtel at the Ritz – an old beanpole who somehow managed to be obsequious and imperious at the same time, who bore the same Christian name as my son, and who was able at a glance to tell a real duke from an impostor, a millionaire from a swindler – sat us at the most fashionable and sought-after table in the place, to the left of the wide hallway that leads to the main dining room. Our neighbours were Noël Coward, dining with a group of RAF officers; Paul-Louis Weiller in dress uniform; Jean Cocteau a little further off, looking sadly hangdog and ignored by the waiter; and Léon-Paul Fargue, who gave us a cordial wave. I made my guest laugh by telling her how, a week earlier as I lunched with the Goncourt jury members at Drouant, her former 'magnificent, noble lion' Sacha had greeted Lucien Descaves with an ironic 'Look who it is!' Decidedly, the war could not be so terrible if even the cowards were back in town, and if we, naïve as we were, still believed (or rather, had decided to believe) in the myth of the blockade and the state of siege that would put an end to Hitler.

I accompanied my exquisite companion to her home and then, on an irresistible impulse, headed for Rue Richer. I parked the car on a dark corner and turned off all the lights. I sat for hours, staring into the night and fighting off sleep. A taxi pulled up towards 1 a.m., and out stepped a nurse in a dark veil and cape. I watched in rigid silence as my daughter-in-law paid the driver and vanished into the courtyard.

I drove straight through the night to Andigny without stopping.

With its soldiers left waiting behind the Maginot Line, my country was waging a pathetic, timorous war, and I couldn't have cared less. Women, too, had become a matter of indifference to me – all but one.

I was madly in love with a Jewess, and this horrendous love was untenable.

I decided to cut myself off from the world and to throw myself wholeheartedly, drawing on every last intellectual resource, into the new book that Bernard Grasset had been pressing me for.

This was *La Grappe mystique*.

I continue to believe that this book, which enjoyed enormous popularity, is the successful synthesis not only of the vagaries of History, but also of the vagaries of my soul and my thought. It ends in a somehow triumphant quietude that is also a sacrifice, though one that can be seen as glorious and selfless. In its prophetic message, it hints at a world neither you nor I will live to see.

On the December morning when I finished it, after a sleepless night spent chained to my desk, the telephone rang. It was the Saint-Jacques hospice.

My wife had just died.

10.

If you remain in the area much longer, Monsieur le Commandant, as I hope you will – where, for a start, will I find a better chess partner? – and your superiors do not send you back to Russia, I will teach you some of the local dialect.

Those glowing bands that furrow the eastern sky just before sunrise – I saw them again this morning – are called *bars of daylight*. Those little blue clouds that stand out against the blue of the sky are *jay wings* (what you call *Häher* or *Holzschreier*). A whirlwind is called a *folly*. The weather is *fattening* or *slimming*, depending on whether there's a threat of rain or the sky is clearing. In the same circumstances, you can also say that the weather is *grieving* or that the sun is *laughing*.

When the soil turns easily, we say it's *obedient*. When a wall or a building is in disrepair, it's *going mad*. Trees can either be *virtuous*, that is, vigorous; *stunned*, stunted or withered; or *furious* when they grow too fast. Very often, they are seen to be *ailering*, or suffering. A good belt of woodland is said to be *bawdy* because it is bold and strapping. Plants that flower magnificently are sometimes called *prideful*, or *cheeky*. The rapid growth of vegetation in the month of May is compared to boiling liquid: the woods *burl*; the explosive growth of the hedgerows is a *burling*.

The spring of 1940 was wonderfully early and beautiful. Was it the same on your side of the Rhine? I don't recall. Here in Normandy and all across France, the sun laughed and our parched hedges did little burling compared to previous years, while without Marguerite to keep it up, the garden slowly died under my exhausted gaze. Day after day, neither bars nor jay wings streaked or speckled the absurdly blue sky, although the thunder of weapons began suddenly to rumble to the north, and later to the east. It had been so hot and dry that the rivers had been reduced to trickles and the fish died belly up in the lukewarm waters of the channels alongside our islands, which could be reached practically without the use of a boat. Such weather greatly favoured your lightning war.

You know more about the breakthrough at Sedan than I do, so I won't bother going over it. Split into two sharp prongs, ten German armoured and six motorised divisions sped westward along a road that our command had deemed unworthy of defending. Seven of those ten Panzer divisions crossed the Ardennes and reached the Meuse in three days. Having so poorly defended the sector, General Corap was stripped of his command and replaced by Giraud, who was captured along with his entire general staff. On 20 May, General Von Kleist's tank corps reached the mouth of the Somme in an almost unimaginable burst of speed, attacking our troops in Belgium from the rear. I listened to this awful news on the wireless. I was humiliated by the collapse, which had, of course, been predictable, but like a few others I had come to hope for a brief and apocalyptic campaign for France that, in bringing Marianne to her festering knees, would lay the foundations for a National Rebirth with the long-awaited return of the Victor of Verdun.

Maréchal Pétain, recalled from Spain in mid-May, was appointed Vice-President by Paul Reynaud, and Weygand replaced Gamelin as Supreme Commander. Wladimir d'Ormesson wrote in *Le Matin*: 'The Pétain–Weygand partnership exudes a sense of immense calm. Their names represent such a wealth of experience, wisdom, knowledge, resolve and, ultimately, glory, that they inspire confidence in and of themselves.' In fact, however, the two men despise one another; while their political ideas and their hatred of Bolshevism are as one, they are temperamental opposites. The Maréchal is a wise, serene and prudent man, and above all a miserly spender of French blood, as he demonstrated countless times during the Great War, for instance in 1917 when he put an end to the pointless Nivelle offensive and spared so many mutineers from the firing squad. Weygand, by contrast, is restless – the very picture of that dry, martial and impetuous French officer whose recklessness can lead his troops just as easily to victory as to destruction.

We had heard nothing further from Olivier (last seen at Marguerite's funeral on 29 December). A letter that I sent to him on 1 June, care of his regiment, was returned a few days later with the terse stamp 'Undeliverable'.

Hundreds of refugees from Belgium and Holland had been tramping through our town for weeks, pursuing their futile exodus to the south, a debacle that was accelerated with the fall of Amiens. I was driven to distraction by the sight of this miserable horde from my window, living proof of the anarchy of democracy and the failure of our Western European leaders to prepare appropriately.

As Normandy anticipated attack from the air, measures were taken to protect the civilian population. Monsieur Duplessis, the Mayor, drew up a list of cellars that could serve as air-raid shelters, enacted public lighting regulations, and ordered automobile headlights to be painted blue.

In order to gather more information, on 6 June I went to Paris, where I lunched with Monsieur de Lequerica, the Spanish Ambassador. He had held several private meetings with the Maréchal over recent days. The latter had acknowledged his belief that he was the man for the job, but that President Lebrun, a puppet in the hands of the parties, would not offer him the reins of power, while on the other hand a coup d'état – the only other way to secure them – was a serious matter that one did not consider lightly. The Maréchal doubted, too, that his voice would be heard by Chancellor Hitler if he offered peace talks. The Ambassador explained to me that this confession had been of great interest to the Spanish Minister for Foreign Affairs, who had brought it to the attention of General Franco. The latter had in turn offered Maréchal Pétain (his erstwhile teacher at the École de Guerre), via the intermediary of the Ambassador with whom I was lunching, a direct connection to the Führer. Spain, fearing the spread of a conflict that it wanted nothing to do with – its army having been bled white, and its government finding its forceful allies in Berlin and Rome more burdensome than anything else – wanted a rapid return to peace on its borders. I went home with the sense that Pétain was finally preparing himself to answer the call!

Ilse and Hermione arrived at Andigny station the following day, Friday the 7th, with no prior warning. At table, my daughter-in-law, who was no longer in uniform, told me what had happened. On 26 May, her ambulance, attached to the light cavalry corps, was caught under German fire at Haubourdin, in the north, and another nurse, her friend Germaine Colliard, had been killed. Ilse had been lucky to escape the planes. I trembled as I listened to her account. Her unit was scattered. Knowing first-hand the strength of the Germans and convinced that the war was already lost, Ilse had been concerned for Hermione and had returned to Paris by her own means to collect her daughter. We listened to the wireless together. Reading between the lines of the falsely reassuring reports, I gathered that Weygand, attacked on the Somme and the Aisne, was falling back under the weight of your divisions, and that the Royal Air Force had betrayed us. Paul Reynaud had reshuffled his government, but nothing could now contain the military and moral catastrophe. I sensed that our soldiers had succumbed to panic, which could not fail to spread like a flame on a trail of gunpowder. I fiddled with the radio dial until I found Radio Stuttgart. On the German airwaves, the old-time actor

Obrecht, otherwise known as Saint-Germain, cackled as he read the lines prepared for him by Paul Ferdonnet, whom I had known at *La Victoire* and the Parti Socialiste National and who had already gone over to the enemy.

'The Luftwaffe will be over the Seine valley by tomorrow! People of Andigny, get ready for a hot old time! Ha ha ha!'

Ilse sat beside me and groaned, while over there in Stuttgart your announcer burst into laughter like a pantomime villain.

That evening, a journalist friend telephoned me from Forges-les-Eaux. He was sitting at his dining-room window, looking at dust-covered German tanks parked pretty as you please beneath the trees in the square! As you know, Forges is only sixty kilometres from Andigny. Two armoured divisions from Hoth's motorised corps, which had been thought to still be in Flanders, had launched an all-out assault against the Hornoy plateau, broken our lines and made a dash for the south! This astounding, tragic news meant that the road to Rouen was now open. And once Normandy had fallen, Paris would be caught in the pincers. From a strategic point of view, our little town, straddling one of the main bends of the Seine between Rouen and Vernon, was now an important objective for your high command. An aerial attack was therefore more than likely to be expected as early as the next day. My daughter-in-law begged me to help her escape. She was terrified of the Nazis, and I knew why.

I had been stockpiling cans of petrol in the garage for some time. While Ilse and Hermione took a brief nap – I planned to leave at dawn – I filled the tank of my Rochet-Schneider, loaded another fifty litres in the back, fully inflated the tyres and checked the pressure on the spare. In imitation of the refugees, I tied a mattress on the roof to protect us from strafing. From my desk I retrieved two handguns: my old 1892 Lebel regulation revolver, which had served me faithfully in the Great

War, and for my daughter-in-law a 1928 Le Français 9 mm automatic. I would rely on these weapons more for show than to return fire, as I anticipated more problems with the vanquished than with the victors. Subsequent events were to prove me right.

To bolster my status, I donned my commandant's uniform, including my Légion d'Honneur and 1914–1918 Croix de Guerre medals, and slipped into my cavalry boots. I woke Ilse and the little one at six, and we drank coffee. I told my daughter-in-law to wear her nurse's uniform, which, in conjunction with my officer's dress, might prove useful in getting us past certain obstacles. I intended to leave at daybreak, in the cool of early morning, while the stragglers of the exodus, whose cars and wagons clogged our main street and church square, were still asleep and would thus be less likely to delay our departure.

Our bags were light by necessity, as the heavy petrol cans occupied a good deal of space. I had nevertheless packed rain gear and blankets, and provisions for two or three days. I anticipated that we would often have to sleep outdoors or in the car, which, for as long as it continued to run, we would need to keep a close eye on.

At the first glimmer of dawn, I had just opened the doors of the garage overlooking the riverbank when the grim howling of air-raid sirens came to life. I watched as the first green and grey planes appeared from beyond the hills bordering the Vexin plateau, their wings marked with black crosses.

With all the fuel they contained, my car and the garage posed a terrible danger should they be hit by bullets or even a single bomb. I grabbed Ilse and Hermione by the hand and we ran for the marina. From the shelter of the pier, we saw the planes – your Stukas with their distinctive wings, leading a squadron of light bombers – follow the crest of the hills then veer right towards the centre of town, passing beyond the castle and disappearing from view. A moment later we heard the booming of the first bombs, which definitively silenced the panic-stricken wails of the siren.

I estimated that we had a few minutes before the second wave of the attack. We ran back to the car. I got behind the wheel and started the engine, zigzagging along the embankment between the refugee vehicles and carts, whose owners were just waking up, throwing terrified glances at the sky. I ordered Ilse, who sat beside me, to hold on to her weapon and display it if necessary. Hermione, sitting behind us, was torn between fear and exhilaration. To our left, an immense column of smoke rose into the sky: the heart of Andigny was aflame. I could barely hear the distant rumbling of the squadron, which was undoubtedly executing a wide U-turn above the plateau.

Having passed the last houses, I crossed the old bridge, which the town regiment, barracked at the École Militaire, had not yet blown up. Hermione, peeking through the rear window, cried out that the 'Boche planes' were coming back; indeed, their roar was deafening as they passed quite high above our car. Once we reached the other side of the river, I pushed the accelerator to the floor. Bombs rained down far behind us, and I saw new plumes of smoke rising in the rear-view mirror. After driving along rural back roads for a quarter of an hour, we came in sight of Gaillon, which was in total chaos. The fleeing vehicles had blocked a column of our motorised infantry, and as soon as I could I headed out across the fields in a cloud of dust. We thereby reached the Evreux road, the only route leading south-west to a bridge across the Eure.

I was overtaken by a strange sense of joy when the car crossed that serene little structure, lined with weeping willows overhanging the calm, marshy waters. I finally had a chance to *act*! Olivier was far away, unable to protect his wife and little girl. As a French officer, I felt myself fully worthy to do so in his place. The ongoing disaster – an anomaly steeped in mediocrity – was to be blamed on the mistakes of the French, not on the genius of their Motherland. For France,

Monsieur le Commandant, is only truly herself when summoned to the highest of duties; that is when the *furia francese* courses through the veins of her soldiers, and France becomes once again *la France* in all her grandeur.

11.

In the words of Michelet, Monsieur le Commandant, France is not a *race*, in the strict sense of the word; it is a *people*.

To be sure, there is no point in denying that the French Nation was created in successive waves. The Greco-Latin civilisation, and later the Christian, were built atop the ancient Celtic or Gaulish foundation. In the fifth century after Jesus Christ, the Gallo-Romans were in turn submerged by the Visigoths, the Burgundians, and above all the Franks.

The millennial layers do not disappear for all that, but the civilisations and ethnic groups have blended one with another over the centuries. Materially, certain physical and juridical traits of the Franks tend to dominate, at least north of the Loire; at the moral and religious levels, it is above all the traditions and sensibility of the Greco-Latins that have shaped the French soul. As to the Gaulish temperament, passionate and generous, it will live forever!

To this Gallo-Roman-Frankish scaffolding we must add those provinces that were part of ancient Gaul, and are indisputably incorporated into French geographic territory, but are peopled with independent races: the Bretons, the Basques, the Catalans, the Allobroges, and so on.

The miracle lies in the fact that, thanks to the policies of our kings – centralising and regionalist in equal measure – all these ethnic layers have been fused in the common crucible and have adopted, if not the same physical type, customs and tastes that are at least very similar.

The Frenchman approaches his work with enthusiasm, as he does all his undertakings. Historically, our people were the pioneers of every chivalric mission. In the Middle Ages, moved by the populist fervour embodied in Peter the Hermit, we invented the Crusades, and participated at the forefront of each and every one. In the eighteenth century we crusaded again, not against the Muslims but for the notion of liberty – an abstract and anarchic chimera, perhaps, but the Frenchman has a need to defend a higher cause, and to compel the rest of Europe to join in. In the nineteenth century, the Frenchman crusaded for all the altruistic ideals: the beautiful and the just, which gave rise to his missionary and charitable work; and the utopian, such as Equality and Fraternity.

To satisfy his sense of honour and his need for something larger than himself, the Frenchman introduced the concept of Chivalry. Regardless of the nobility of his birth, the Frenchman was a born Knight in his respect for maidens, widows and all those weaker than himself (the Jews cleverly exploited this national trait to drag us into their war by persuading us to come to Poland's assistance); in staying true to his own word; and in his penchant for selfless gestures and even futile loyalties.

My gesture may have been selfless – if my daughter-in-law had not come to plead for my help, I would undoubtedly have stayed at home, contemptuous of the mass flight – but I counted on my efforts to bear fruit. The night had given me leisure to gather my thoughts and study the map. Avoiding Chartres and Le Mans (which could very well be quickly overrun in the event that Paris, sensing the German pincer about to close, abruptly gave way to panic), I decided to pursue our south-westerly route as directly as possible. And if the front continued to advance, and the rout deteriorated further, we could head southwards all the way to the Pyrenees. I had, and still have, good friends in Spain, both in the General Staff and the diplomatic corps. It also occurred to me that I could make use of Maréchal Pétain's contacts, since he was a fellow Academy member and a personal friend of General Franco's, and had made the best of impressions in Madrid. Having decided to remain neutral in the midst of the European upheavals, Spain could serve as a temporary safe haven for Ilse if she was really so terrified of the Germans.

From Evreux, which we were obliged to circumvent, we reached Conches and the Ouche region, whose jittery population was packing up and readying to flee in its turn. Other runaways were arriving en masse from Vexin. The more the morning advanced, the more the roads grew clogged with vehicles of all sorts, while the village bells rang out the alarm everywhere continually. The wind of panic was blowing across my lovely farming country, thrown headlong and unsuspecting into war and exodus. Our farmers now joined the horde of northerners – Dutch, Belgians and Picards – who had been streaming by for days under their mocking or compassionate gaze. The situation was deteriorating from one hour to the next. The road to Verneuil-sur-Avre was already considerably congested with carts, horses and automobiles; that to Alençon, it seemed to me, was at a complete standstill.

Disorganised units of the Tenth Army were pulling back, before having made any contact with the enemy, to join the chaotic tide of deserters of all ages and social classes. We encountered a long column of French military, led by light tanks that advanced with a grinding metallic noise, followed by a convoy of ambulances and mobile artillery, and an endless file of trucks in camouflage at the rear. Shortly afterwards, some thirty kilometres to our left, your air force pounded a military airfield, pulverising our planes on the ground and blowing up the fuel depots. Vast columns of black smoke rose above abandoned fields, where cows ran back and forth mooing in desperate concert, begging to be milked. The stench of burning permeated the air, adding to the stifling heat. We had not brought enough water and Hermione was already complaining of thirst. I stopped at a farmhouse, where without compunction they charged us three francs a litre for well water.

Outraged by the peasants' greed, the refugees returned the favour by blithely helping themselves to fruit and vegetables in the field. In the small towns, I saw smashed windows and grocers' shops looted by the crowds. I noted that even the disbanded soldiers participated in these misdeeds. At the wheel of our overladen car, now pinioned in one great traffic jam, I raged at the unprecedented spectacle of my country's sudden abasement. A collective madness had taken hold of France and the French. All our values seemed to have been cast into the gutter, creating a disgusting flotsam caught up in a vortex of selfishness, impotence, chaos, defeatism, anger, stupidity, incoherence, submission, cupidity, cowardice, drunkenness, rancour, hatred and resignation, all in the tragic turmoil of a vast, incomprehensible and uncontrolled scramble to safety, every man for himself.

These Frenchmen that I have described, Monsieur le Commandant, this heroic people – I no longer recognised them. As I later came to understand, their fall was merely the reflection of a deeper corruption: the evil had taken root in the very depths of our men; it had entered their bloodstreams. It had undermined their souls to an extent that none had dared to imagine, and it had taken this collapse to reveal the damage in all its tragic scope.

If our victorious Army of the Great War had thrown in the towel a mere four weeks into the assault, it was not only the result of the enemy's superior manpower and weaponry. It was because the French Army, like the Nation from which it emanated, had also been eroded by a terrible leprosy.

Ever since its victory in 1918, France had never ceased to dodge, to scheme, to close its eyes to the developments around it. In an unforgivable abandonment of resolve, it had consistently refused to rise to any effort, to make the least sacrifice; it had been content merely to enjoy itself, relying on others to provide it with the means. It had opted for ease, illusion, delirium, anything rather than labour for its own salvation.

Need I add that any country that abandons itself to such impulses is irremediably doomed to suffer the worst forms of servitude?

12.

I decided to bear west, heading for Argentan via L'Aigle. This route was clear, being perpendicular to the direction of the exodus, and once we had broken from the horde it took us only half an hour to reach L'Aigle, where we ate in the dining room of a hotel packed with travellers. The radio thundered out the latest news: the Tenth Army had abandoned Versailles and pulled back towards Alençon, where it would join forces with General Héring's Sixth Army and General Frère's Seventh to form a new defensive front along a line stretching from Caen through Alençon and Fontainebleau to Sens.

I estimated that, at that time, we were only one or two days ahead of the enemy. That was not even counting his air force, whose raids could strike deep into our territory and whose Stukas, it was said, did not hesitate to strafe columns of civilians mercilessly. Our fighter force with its outdated Moranes paled by comparison, while the English had perfidiously deserted the skies, opting for a cautious withdrawal to their island while they waited to see how the situation would play out. We ate quickly and struck out again to the west, passing two Hotchkiss tanks that had been abandoned by the side of the road for lack of fuel. In Nonant-le-Pin, we had the devil of a time crossing the monstrous flow of vehicles heading south along the main road: trucks; ambulances; cars of all ages, their roofs covered in mattresses, their interiors chock-a-block with the most ridiculous cargo of brooms, hat boxes, birdcages, bundles of laundry and silverware, not to mention pets; carts loaded with pathetic, haphazard possessions; exhausted packhorses; motorcycles; sidecars; bikes; tandems; perambulators and even wheelbarrows. The poorest trudged on foot at the sides of the road, harassed and covered in dust. I had to honk my horn, shout, order people to make way. I pretended that I needed to reach my unit, which drew oaths and insults. The masses considered all officers to be cowards. 'We're done for because of you!' one man yelled in the midst of a chorus of catcalls. I sped up as fists rained down on the roof and spittle splattered the windows. Hermione was crying, while Ilse sought to reassure her with calming words; once again, I could only admire her sangfroid.

Since the Argentan road veered north-west, as soon as I was able I turned left onto a by-road that led into the Orne valley, deep into a delightful, bucolic landscape where the war seemed to belong to another time, another world.

I stopped the Rochet-Schneider on a shady hillside. The fuel gauge indicated an almost empty tank and I brought out two cans to fill it up, sheltered from the covetous stares of passers-by. My passengers stepped away to relieve themselves. I studied the map. We would soon reach the northernmost stretch of the Écouves forest; passing through Rânes would bring us to La Ferté-Macé, a major junction where we could turn south towards Mayenne and Laval while skirting Alençon and avoiding the main road to Le Mans, which I had no doubt was already clogged with traffic. I hoped to cross the Loire somewhere between Tours and Nantes.

In the little town of Rânes, a petrol station was still selling fuel, one can per person, and some fifty cars were already queuing at the pump. I had seen much worse on our journey: many tanks in the area had already been drained dry, while people were forced to wait hours in the sun at those that had not. We still had a long way to go to reach the Loire, and I thought it wise to stop here and fill one of the two cans that I had emptied. We had been waiting some twenty minutes when a group of five or six infantrymen falling back from Argentan

– I knew they were deserters, as they were without their rifles – took notice of my car, the most luxurious in the queue. They approached us hurling the most vulgar insults, among them the allegation that I was one of those officers who had 'sold us to the Boches' and that I was sneaking off to the Côte d'Azur with my nurse, who they claimed – pointing and laughing at the terrified child in the back of the car – was obviously not only an unmarried mother but a soldier's tart.

They clearly intended to make off with our car in order to speed their flight from the enemy. I could see bottles sticking out of the pockets of their coats, and their breath reeked of alcohol.

I had time neither to protest nor to take up my weapon to defend myself. The drunken deserters pulled me from the car and began to pummel and kick me as I rolled in the dust. I heard Hermione scream shrilly. A shot rang out, and the beating suddenly stopped.

I saw, among the mud-caked combat boots and legs wrapped in khaki puttees, two elegant shoes topped with black hose, and the hem of a white dress. Ilse had fired a warning shot in the air and was now pointing her automatic at the thugs. 'Leave my father alone,' she cried. 'What kind of cowards hit an old man, a disabled veteran? It's because of shirkers like you that we're losing the war!' The soldiers, deflated and shamefaced, ran off without another word. My daughter-in-law, followed by several drivers who had watched the beating without lifting a finger, came and helped carry me to the shade of a plane tree. It hurt me to breathe, I had a nasty cut over my eyebrow, I could feel my face begin to swell, and my nose dripped with blood.

Unable to drive, I suggested that Ilse take the wheel, but she was alarmed by my condition and determined that I should not attempt to travel in the prevailing hazardous circumstances. She went to speak to the owner of a café that rented out rooms, and although the establishment was fully booked, he agreed, for thirty francs a night, to let us have a room in the shed at the bottom of the garden. I was carried there and passed out, awaking an hour later to find myself being examined by a doctor. The little country town had not given in to panic, and most of the locals, more afraid of being looted by the refugees than of being aggressed by the German troops, had chosen to remain in their houses and farms. I had two broken ribs and several contusions.

We spent eight days in Rânes, where my daughter-in-law cared for me with admirable devotion. The room was furnished with a big old peasant bed, and the café owner's wife had a cot brought in for Hermione. It was in this way that circumstances led me, for the first time in my life, to share a bed with my son's spouse.

I was barely aware of this development on the first night, having succumbed to a high fever. The past and the present intermingled in my consciousness; I spoke to Marguerite, to Jeanne, and when I came to I found myself trembling with humiliation. I had been incapable of protecting the person I loved; rather, it had been she who had saved us by putting our attackers to flight, calling me an 'old man' and claiming me as her father.

Her father. Was that how Ilse thought of me? I considered this question for the first time. In the eyes of the German, of the Jewess, was I a substitute for her own father, lost somewhere in Berlin or Palestine, and perhaps dead? Was the affection in which the young woman clearly held me merely – I say 'merely', though it was undoubtedly deeply as well – a filial one?

I had lost Jeanne, my precious child, but had not the Lord in His infinite goodness compensated me with the love and presence of a second daughter?

If that were the case, the 'amorous' love that I experienced for her in such an incandescent way was an abominable and blasphemous one.

In the middle of the night I burst into hysterical laughter; my bedfellow thought that I was delirious. I heard the roof timbers creaking in the wind, the wood cracking; my body was racked with trembling, and my hair stood on end. I tossed and turned, the sheets damp with my sweat, a taste of ashes in my mouth and nausea rising in my belly, my guts in knots. I was back in the trenches; shells whistled overhead and churned the martyred earth. The sky was yellow. I found myself once again in the 'ravine of death' between Douaumont and Vaux. Branchless tree trunks pointing at the sky. A donkey struck down, half-eaten by dogs; headless German corpses. I pushed back the sheets, raised my fist and cried out to the Almighty: 'He who created ears, will He not hear me without ears? He who created eyes, will He not see me without eyes?' A nurse in a white veil held me by the shoulders, begged me to remain calm. Sobbing, I called her Jeanne. 'Jeanne, my darling girl, you have returned from the dead ...'

Ilse turned away, and I heard her crying.

13.

The fever broke after three days.

To the north, the roar of cannon fire drew nearer.

The hordes of refugees continued to stream through town, heading west and south.

From my bed, I could hear the popular songs being played on the wireless in the main dining room. Danielle Darrieux was a regular feature:

> My first is a tender glance,
> My second is a mocking smile,
> My third, the words I long to hear,
> And my whole lies inside my heart.

On the evening of Tuesday the 11th, we heard the sound of aeroplane engines. Supported by my nurse, I went out into the garden. A bomber was approaching from the south at low altitude. The plane was swerving in distress, long orange flames leaping from its wings and cockpit. There was a crackling sound. The pilot seemed to be desperately searching for a place to land. Night was falling, and I was unable to make out the aircraft's markings, but in any case I did not see the Luftwaffe's black crosses on the undersides of its wings.

The bomber passed by in a deafening roar only twenty metres overhead. I thought I saw figures silhouetted against the flames. A stink of burning filled the air above the garden, where we stood with our eyes turned to the deep-blue sky, still bright in the west, while Ilse held me steady with her left arm around my waist. The plane disappeared from sight, the noise of the engines receded, rose, then receded again. A few minutes later there was an explosion, followed by a brief orange flash to the north-west. Ilse's grip tightened on my flesh, her shivering body pressed against mine, then she leaned her head towards me and I felt her hair on my neck. I draped my one arm around her shoulders, and we stayed that way for several minutes without speaking. Then we returned to the shed, where Hermione slept undisturbed.

The next morning, the café owner told us that the plane had fallen at La Boulardière, near Orgères, and that one wing had been found as far away as La Brousse. Some locals had gone in little groups to see the wreckage. It was an English Whitney bomber. Five bodies had been found inside, charred beyond recognition. A torn parachute hung across a hedgerow. French soldiers from a regiment temporarily garrisoned in Gacé were guarding the site, where an army interpreter had recovered the flight plans. The plane had taken off from Jersey on a night bombing mission to Turin, in response to Mussolini's declaration of war. It may have been hit by defensive anti-aircraft fire while crossing the front line. Ilse suggested that in the general confusion those poor Englishmen, who had been coming from the south when we saw them, had been hit by our people, and had turned back in an attempt to get home.

In the following days, a great number of French troops poured in from the west to take up positions in the region and face the German divisions that had overrun the Fontainebleau forest. The 3rd Armoured Car Regiment set up headquarters between Rânes and La Ferté-Macé. We were torn between leaving, and running the risk of being caught on the road in the midst of fighting, and staying at the café, at the mercy of the bombs.

Day after day I put off making the decision until the morrow, while in reality I was savouring my nights of burning intimacy with my daughter-in-law. I did not allow myself to touch or even brush against her, in spite of her proximity and my desire, but I felt her warmth, inhaled her scent, and listened to her breathing in the night so close at hand, and sometimes moaning in restless slumber. My heart beat faster when I heard her sweet groans, and I felt my hardened member pulse for her.

On 17 June, with cannon fire in the near distance, a large crowd of locals gathered in the main dining room of the café to hear an important announcement on the radio. At 12.30 p.m., the Maréchal began his speech; his voice sounded oddly weak to me. It's true that the Victor of Verdun was eighty-four years old that day when destiny decreed that he should be called a second time to the salvation of his Motherland.

> People of France, at the request of the President of the Republic, as of today I have assumed leadership of the government. Convinced of the devotion in which I am held by our admirable army, which is fighting with a heroism worthy of its historic military traditions against an enemy superior in numbers and weaponry; convinced that in its magnificent resistance it has fulfilled its obligations to its allies; convinced of the support of the veterans whom I have had the honour to command, today I consecrate myself to France to attenuate her misfortune …

A clamour erupted, punctuated by diverse commentary, a few shouts of 'Long live Pétain!', including my own, loud and clear: 'Long live Pétain!'

The speech continued: 'It is with a heavy heart that I tell you today to lay down your weapons. I contacted the enemy last night to ask whether he is ready to discuss with us …'

Loud sobs rang out on all sides, and when I turned to Ilse, I saw that her German cheeks, too, were bathed in tears.

The Maréchal's address ended soon afterwards, but the remainder was drowned out in the uproar, and the 'Marseillaise' was broadcast on the wireless immediately thereafter. Those who had been sitting rose to their feet, and the entire crowd stood to attention. At that moment, every single person in that café in Rânes – man or woman, young or old – was in tears.

An angry rumbling was heard outside on the square, and we watched as a convoy of French military vehicles overran the town centre in a cloud of dust. A section of 75 mm guns took up position. An officer burst into the café and ordered all civilians to drop everything they were doing and evacuate westward, towards Saint-Fraimbault, or else to seek shelter in their cellars. A decisive battle was about to take place in the area. The café owner's wife protested that Maréchal Pétain had just announced a ceasefire.

In a tone that admitted no rejoinder, the officer replied that he was squadron leader Jacques Weygand, the son of Maréchal Weygand, that his father would never capitulate in the midst of a campaign, that he had received no order to cease fire, that Pétain was known for his defeatism, and that here the French Army would fight to the very last man.

The captain's fierce pride reminded me of myself in my youth, and I admired it despite the fact that Pétain's rise to power had been my deepest wish, and that I was convinced that the way forward he had proposed was the only one that made any sense.

I took Ilse by the arm and announced that we had to leave Rânes without delay. The café owner had parked the Rochet-Schneider in his garage. I settled with that good man, and he and his wife helped to gather our belongings and pack the car. Hermione resumed her place in the back. The 75s deployed at the edge of town began to fire with a terrible racket. On the square, two wounded cavalry soldiers informed Captain Weygand that a sizeable column of motorised German infantry was approaching, and the captain ordered a young tank commander to go out to meet them.

As we left Rânes in a long, slow-moving file of trucks, cars and carts, from the top of a hill we saw unfold the Dantesque spectacle of a column of German tanks some five or six kilometres to the north-east, moving openly and flying little white pennants. The Panzers drove before them a scattered crowd of refugees, who ran with their hands up, abandoning their luggage, amidst dust-covered automobiles weaving across the fields, units of infantrymen who had fallen back from the failed attempt to cross the Orne, and disarmed soldiers from both sides whom the combatants caught up in the fighting had neglected to take prisoner. Shells exploded in the midst of this vast chaos, fortunately without doing great harm, while the fleeing figures continued to run in our direction as the column of Panzers closed in.

I watched the battle helplessly, mesmerised by the action. To the east, I saw three of our armoured vehicles moving along the groves and hedges, two on one side and one on the other, concealed from the view of a column of some forty German troop carriers. Your helmeted soldiers, clustered at the back of the trucks and unaware of the rapid approach of our light tanks, were singing at the top of their lungs. The wind carried snippets of their song all the way to us.

The three tanks turned abruptly to take the column from the rear. One pulled up directly behind the last truck and fired on it point-blank, sending mutilated bodies into the air. At my side, Ilse let out a cry. The tanks now ran alongside the column at full speed, blowing up the carriers one after the other and machine-gunning those who tried to flee. By the time we came to a bend in the road that blocked our view of the fighting all around Rânes, the entire column of trucks was nothing but a vast smoking ruin of blackened iron and shredded corpses.

We ran across a motorcycle platoon leading tanks to the defence of La Ferté-Macé. Clearly, in spite of the Maréchal's call to lay down arms, a terrible clash was in the making for the Orne and the Mayenne – perhaps the last fighting of the French campaign. The motorcyclists sped on towards Carrouges, while our car moved off in the opposite direction. Hermione managed to sleep despite all the gunfire, and my daughter-in-law turned to cover her with a blanket.

Later, towards dusk, having found protection behind the lines of the Tenth Army, which continued to fall back towards Brittany with the aim of defending a hypothetical 'Breton enclave', with heavy hearts and tear-filled eyes we contemplated in the dying light the vast, dark oceans of the Andaines and Écouves forests. In the distance flames rose from bombed villages: Rânes, Carrouges, Saint-Georges-d'Annebecq, while in Saint-Fraimbault the last of our heroic troops, remnants of the 3rd Mobile Artillery Regiment and the 13th Light Motorised Brigade that had been attacked from all sides, were reduced to surrender.

14

We resumed our journey southward, for I had not given up on my plan to cross the Loire.

The horrendous spectacle of defeat was all around us. The roadside verges were strewn with abandoned vehicles, the bodywork battered, windows smashed and chassis dismantled, stripped of their wheels, engines and anything serviceable. Some cars bore the scars of German strafing: little oblong holes across their roofs; their seats and banquettes stained with large brown puddles of dried blood. At the side of the road we saw little hillocks of freshly turned earth, topped with a tragic cross hurriedly assembled with branches. Haphazard objects, knick-knacks, toys, boxes, suitcases, waterlogged papers, rags and torn clothing littered the ground between carts with broken axles or shafts, ambulances scorched by fire, dead horses with great hunks of flesh torn away, exposing the white ribs, broken-down motorcycles with their sidecars, bicycle frames without wheels, overturned perambulators, empty trailers, burned tyres, abandoned field kitchens ...

There were rumours circulating that the Germans had already crossed the Loire; that many bridges had been destroyed to slow the enemy's progress; that, on the contrary, General Griveaud, commander of the Eleventh Region, had refused to blow up the bridges of the city he had been assigned to defend; that all towns of more than 20,000 inhabitants had been declared open cities by the new government; that the Italian air force was bombing Orléans, Blois, Tours, Saumur, Angers. The localities through which we passed were awash with white flags. In Craon, some sixty kilometres short of Angers, we were told that France had been divided into two zones, and that the Germans would forbid us from crossing the demarcation line. Our flight, all the risks we had taken, had been in vain. The only thing left to do was to return to Paris.

At a restaurant in Château-Gontier where we stopped for lunch, I encountered someone I knew, Josyane C., a proofreader at my publishing house. The young woman had fled Paris with her mother, a most distinguished lady who would now have to find her own way back to Paris, while Mademoiselle C. was determined to push on for Spain, and from there to join up with de Gaulle, whom she had heard broadcast a radio appeal for the war to be pursued from across the Channel. As the British would no doubt be suing for peace soon enough – they were merely raising the stakes in order to secure better conditions than those to which the extent of our own defeat had exposed us – I thought that this was an utterly unrealistic and even anti-French prospect that was doomed to utter failure. I nevertheless invited Madame C. to join us, making room next to Hermione by jettisoning the empty petrol cans.

In mid-afternoon of the following day we reached Le Mans, now occupied by the Wehrmacht. The tank of the Rochet-Schneider was nearly empty, and we could not take the risk of breaking down in the middle of the countryside. Hundreds of motorists seemed to be in the same situation, and had spread their bedding over the ground in the main square in the centre of town, resigned to camping out in their cars, while a German truck blared Wagner's *Twilight of the Gods* from a loudspeaker mounted on its roof. The tables and chairs of the café terraces lining the square were filled with soldiers and officers in blue-green uniform, while a few women who had hastened to consort with the victor mingled among them.

The merchants of Le Mans had been cleaned out by the flood of people, and we ourselves had exhausted our provisions. Restaurants and hotels all declared themselves full, and the shelves of the grocers' shops were bare. The money I had brought with me from Andigny, hidden beneath my clothes (I had taken the precaution of dressing as a civilian this time, French officers having become quite unpopular of late), was therefore useless to us. All that remained was one bottle of red wine, which we shared with our nearest neighbours in the encampment, an American in his fifties and his companion, a young mulatta from the French Antilles. They readily offered us sandwiches, put together with their last cans of sardines and a loaf of bread that the resourceful American had managed to track down at a local bakery. The couple, who lived in the Paris suburbs, were returning from Les Sables-d'Olonne, where, like us, they had found themselves caught behind the new border. I don't know why, but I told them that I was travelling with 'my wife, my daughter and my mother'. Old Madame C. seemed to find the improvisation amusing, if a little cheeky; Hermione burst out laughing, and my daughter-in-law blushed. I think that, unconsciously, I wanted to avenge myself for the lie she had told during our skirmish in Rânes. If she thought fit to pass me off as her father, I would get back at her by choosing to call her my wife.

The American seemed to be excessively taken by Ilse's beauty. He explained that he was a photographer and would be glad to take her portrait. His heavy Yankee accent was rather comical and somewhat mitigated the earnestness of his proposal. It was still broad daylight at eight o'clock as we emptied the bottle and chatted amiably. Soon the negress and Ilse, always sociable, were calling each other 'Ady' and 'Ilsy'. The photographer, who gave his name as Man Ray, associated with a number of prominent Parisians in the arts and letters, such as Jean Cocteau, whom he boasted of having photographed, as well as Picasso and the couturier Paul Poiret. At the time, I thought that I was dealing with an affable mythomaniac, but I later learned that this good-natured American artist, who ultimately returned to his own country, was telling the truth. He was in with the Surrealist group.

We had a rather heated political argument. Man Ray claimed to be an 'anarchist' and anti-Nazi, whereas I demonstrated that the Maréchal's rise to power was the only way to end the prevailing chaos and to stop the bloodshed. As to those so-called Nazis – in my opinion, they were more likely to be honest peasants or clerks whom Hitler had rallied to the flag – who were dining with all the ingenuousness of tourists, easy-going and jovial despite the exhaustion of campaigning, at the café terraces surrounding the square while regaling us with high-quality music (the American retorted that he hated Wagner) – now that they had won their fight, had they not proven to be remarkably peaceful, merciful and disciplined victors?

The next morning – after a strange night spent under the open sky in the middle of town – I felt someone shake me by the shoulder. It was Man Ray, who told me in a whisper how he had devised a plan to obtain a full tank of petrol for our two cars. All he needed was for me to lend a hand, in exchange for which he would share the fuel with me. The previous day, he had approached two Wehrmacht interpreters for help as the national of a neutral country, and they had agreed to show him where to procure petrol before anyone else, since the distribution to refugees in the Occupied Zone would not begin for several days. We would first leave the square on the pretext of finding a hotel outside town for my family, who were extremely tired. I also had to bring a blanket along to cover the petrol cans.

I got into the American's little car. His girlfriend stayed behind with Ilse, Hermione and Madame C. About ten minutes north of town, at the corner of a little side road, my driving companion found the sign for 'Le Château Bleu' that had been described by the Germans. The way led to a clearing guarded by a sentry, his rifle fixed with a bayonet. The American gave him the password. The soldier knocked at the door of a gatehouse, from which emerged one of the interpreters, in shirtsleeves. The young man got into our car and guided us to another, larger clearing, where we found four enormous English tanks that had been captured in Dunkirk and which the Germans wanted to study. Their fuel reservoirs were full; all we had to do was help ourselves! The interpreter left us to work it out for ourselves and walked back to his gatehouse.

The photographer climbed up to the turret and slipped inside the tank. He managed to get the engine started, proving that there was fuel in the reservoir. Then he shut the machine down. I heard a clicking sound from somewhere beneath the thick armour plating, then Man Ray emerged, looking quite absurd in a radio helmet he had found in the cabin. From the turret, he told me to lift up each of the armour plates one after the other. I found the petrol cap. The American came down, opened it and gave it a sniff. 'First-rate aviation fuel,' he confirmed. Recalling a length of rubber tubing that had been left in the boot of his car, he handed it to me to siphon off the petrol – first into the tank of his car, and then into the cans we had brought along. Some oil cans had been left beside the tanks, and we filled those too. Man Ray thanked the interpreter when we passed the gatehouse on the way out, and presented him with a bottle of champagne that he had brought from Paris. 'Ah, Paris!' your compatriot sighed, and asked for the American's address in expressing his hope that he might pay him a visit on his next leave. Somewhat ungratefully, my driving companion gave him a false name and address, and we returned to Le Mans in a very jolly mood, laden with a good hundred litres of petrol.

It was noon when we got back, and Ilse threw her arms around my neck. She and the others had thought they would never see us again. Her upset was very real, and I was deeply moved by the tears rolling down her cheeks. I almost began to believe in my lie of the day before – that we were husband and wife. Hadn't we been sleeping together for the past two weeks? Man Ray, a decidedly skilful liar, explained to the other refugees gathered around us that we had not found a hotel, but that an old couple living in a bungalow had agreed to rent us two rooms. The lie allowed us to leave the square in two cars without arousing suspicion. I followed close behind the car containing the American and his negress, and once we had left Le Mans behind, we pulled over on a country road to share out our petrol and say our goodbyes. Our friends were heading north like us, but the Surrealist photographer drove like a madman and they soon left us far behind.

We reached Paris without hindrance that evening. The streets of the capital were eerily empty, other than some German trucks. I dropped Madame C. at her home in the Alma district, which was altogether deserted, then drove to Rue Richer, where I intended to sleep at my daughter-in-law's. The concierge gave her an armful of mail, including a letter from Olivier that had arrived that very morning. Ilse opened it, looking more dead than alive. Her face gradually lit up as she read: my son was in the Orléans sector, neither wounded nor captive, and would certainly reach Paris by the next day.

Ilse beamed at me. I should have shared her joy, but a dull bitterness had taken hold of me. I felt as if I had been brutally torn from a dream – a long, marvellous dream – and forced abruptly to see myself as I really was, a lonely old man.

Old man – that was it! In Rânes, confronted by those young men who were beating and rolling me in the dirt, my German daughter-in-law had managed, in French, to hit the nail on the head.

'You'll stay the night with us, of course, Paul-Jean?' she said, pressing the letter to her chest. 'Olivier will be so happy to see you, too.'

I clicked my heels. Trying to attenuate the curtness in my slightly quavering voice, I said, 'Thank you, my child, but I'll be off. I'm a little anxious about the house, you see.'

Refusing the offer of supper, I hugged my family and set off, reaching Andigny shortly before the curfew. The decision to move to German time would not be taken until several days later.

My Villa Némésis was intact, as were the others on the riverside, but all had been requisitioned to house your officers. A helmeted sentry prevented me from entering my own house.

I took a room at the Hôtel Bellevue, where I was well known, and went to bed without supper, feeling deep in my soul, and with unprecedented ferocity, how absurd was this world of ours, and how impenetrable the ways of Our Lord.

15.

The bombs dropped by your Luftwaffe on 8 June, Monsieur le Commandant, spared my home but cruelly ravaged the heart of my city.

All that was left of the beautiful buildings that had surrounded the market square was a pile of smoking ruins. The old Hôtel du Grand Cerf, dating back to Francis I and where Victor Hugo had dined, had gone up in flames from the incendiary bombs. Happily, the town hall, the silk factory and the glassworks had not been touched. Many people, on the morning of the attack, had fled to seek refuge in the neighbouring farms and villages; the rest had cowered in their cellars. There were casualties, whose sorry remains were exhibited in the market square. And some twenty soldiers had died in the fighting at the École Militaire and on their retreat down the former Avenue de la République (now Avenue du Maréchal Pétain), home to the Hôtel de Paris, the headquarters of your Kreiskommandantur. What was left of the French regiment managed to cross the Seine before blowing up the bridge, under fire from your incoming troops.

The first meeting of the Town Council took place on 24 June 1940, a few days after my return to Andigny. In the absence of Mayor Duplessis, who was still in the army, the occupying authorities appointed his secretary, Monsieur Métailié (who would later be so kind as to house me until I was restored to my home), to be his temporary replacement. On 10 July, in the course of a special meeting, eleven new members, including me, were inducted into the new Town Council (the 'Provisional Commission for Communal Administration'). One of our first decisions, adopted unanimously, was, at Monsieur Métailié's suggestion, to reduce to two the number of municipal police officers – who are paid exclusively by the commune, which was already under great strain – assigned to ensure law and order and compliance with the curfew, in collaboration with the Feldgendarmes. Moreover, as a member of the Provisional Commission, I wholeheartedly advocated the timely and effective implementation within our canton of measures with respect to Jewish businesses – the former Sub-Prefect Pierval having called us to order in November concerning the Galeries du Vexin furniture shop, whose owner lives in Lyons-la-Forêt and had failed to put up a sign indicating 'Jewish-owned' in his shop window.

Through my new duties at the town hall and my contact with my fellow citizens and the nearby farmers whom I have known since childhood, I was able to determine that the local population, while still reeling from a rout whose causes, both deep-rooted and immediate, it but poorly understood, was maintaining its dignity. With the exception of the workers who had lost their jobs, the populace resigned themselves with a certain patience to the privations and rigours of the coming months, and valiantly returned to work. The people of Andigny, whose patriotism had emerged revitalised by the ordeal, showed themselves to have faith in the Occupier. However, while they accepted the fait accompli, they nevertheless regretted that one provision of the armistice prevented them from hearing the voice of the French government, to which they remained faithfully devoted and whose declarations they endorsed. Political activity, including that of the trade unions, had come to a standstill. *Le Journal d'Andigny*, which is run by our friend Madame de Feuquerolles, soon resumed publication, continuing to vigorously promote nationalist ideas. Over the course of those months spent restoring order, I noted with satisfaction that the German military authorities generally worked hard to support the French administration, fully recognising the utility of its efforts and the necessity of its involvement, which were in the interests of Germany itself.

In early August, I wrote a letter to Maréchal Pétain in Vichy, having the honour of knowing him personally in our capacities as fellow members of the Academy. I assured him of my deepest respect and unswerving support, and asked that my house be restored to me. I pointed out that I had long been among those who had dearly sought his return to government to save France from the abyss into which we had seen it sinking. And, in offering the services of my pen, I made a number of suggestions, including that of establishing a single party.

I also wrote: 'The rebirth of France through work cannot be effected without the institution of a new social order based on trust and cooperation between owners and workers. *This new social order must overthrow the old way of doing things* – the policy of deal-making with Masonic, capitalist and international elements that has brought us to our current pass. The falling birth rate has compelled us to defend our territory with an unacceptably high ratio of North Africans, colonials and foreigners. *The French family must be restored to its place of honour.* The tide of materialism that overwhelmed France, the spirit of pleasure-seeking and ease are the deep-seated causes of our weakness and our surrender. We must return to the worship and practice of the ideal summarised in these few words: *God, Homeland, Family, Work.* The education of our young people must be reformed.'

I included with the letter a freshly printed copy of *La Grappe mystique*, dedicated to our Leader.

A week later, I received, care of Monsieur Métailié, a handwritten response *from Maréchal Pétain himself.* He thanked me for sending my book (which he looked forward to reading as soon as his labours at the bedside of our defeated and ailing Motherland allowed), and assured me that he had taken the necessary steps for the use of my home to be restored to me: the Secretary of the Academy would send a request on the Maréchal's behalf to the commander of the occupying forces. And he added:

> Many of your ideas, my dear Husson, have hit their mark. As you suggest, we must bring together a group of like-minded thinkers. What we choose to call ourselves is of little import. All true Frenchmen must stand up and be counted. We entirely share your way of thinking. France must revive an ideal that the proliferation of political parties has led her to forget or underestimate. She must revive a conscience that a lack of responsibility has deadened. She must revive a heart that individualism has atrophied or hypertrophied ...[5]

Of course, I was hardly alone among my fellow academicians in proclaiming fervent support for the Maréchal. Not long afterwards, Claudel composed his splendid *Ode to Pétain*:

> France, hear this old man, who thinks of everything and talks to you like a father.
> Daughter of Saint Louis, listen and ask: Have you had your fill of politics yet?
> Hear that steady voice as it proposes and explains its proposals like oil and its truths like gold ...

As soon as I regained possession of Villa Némésis – which Dr Hild, who had been living there, returned graciously and in impeccable condition – I telephoned Rue Richer to invite my family to spend a few days in Andigny. I missed my daughter-in-law. Olivier answered the phone. He sounded awkward, and said that he wanted to talk to me face to face first. Ilse and Hermione could come later in the summer – that could wait. So my son arrived alone, by train. He insisted on talking to me in my office, beyond earshot of the servants. I offered him a chair, and listened to what he had to say, or rather to request.

He began by mentioning the law of 22 July: had I heard of it? I had, and had thought of it myself, but I pretended not to understand why Olivier should want to discuss it with me. As you may be aware, one of the new laws enacted in the summer of 1940, laying the foundations for a complete overhaul of the naturalisation procedures in force since 1927, stipulated that French citizenship could be revoked by decree upon the recommendation of a commission whose membership and functions were to be determined by the Minister of Justice. Olivier was visibly worried about Ilse, whose naturalisation in 1935 would inevitably be reconsidered, one day or another, by the aforesaid review commission.

I raised my eyebrow and asked, 'Do you know of any reason why your wife's French citizenship might not be confirmed?'

My son looked flustered. 'No, but …'

I was playing with Olivier as a cat plays with a mouse: one takes one's revenge where one can.

'Well then,' I said. He said nothing. I went on. 'The law does not specify particular causes for revocation, other than if citizenship has been acquired "for opportunistic reasons" or to rectify past errors. Is there any chance that the commission will learn something about your wife that could prove to be a problem?'

Olivier reddened and mumbled. I felt sorry for him. I had, in fact, already given the matter some serious thought. I knew what had to be done to protect Ilse from the anti-Jewish regulations that I was convinced would soon enter into force, and with a new severity that in any case I approved of in principle. I rose, approached my son, and placed my hand on his shoulder.

'You know that I'm on good terms with the Prefect of Police, Langeron. He and I are in the same social circle; he reads my books. I will call him and request an interview, which he will grant me. He is a cultured, courteous and conscientious civil servant, and will certainly know how to avoid having your wife's file re-opened. Even if my efforts are unnecessary, since as you say, there is *no problem*.'

Impervious to irony, Olivier raised a radiant face to me and clasped my hand with gratitude.

'That's wonderful, Father! It will be such a comfort to me, when I …' He hesitated.

'When you?' I echoed.

He kept my hand in his and, staring me in the eye, said in an exalted tone: 'When I go away. It's all decided, you see. I'm leaving with a friend. We have a connection. We'll go first to Spain, and then by boat to London!'

So the idiot was planning to join de Gaulle! I asked him frostily if he, too, was determined to be condemned to death. To see himself stripped of the citizenship that he hoped to preserve for his wife, a foreigner. And he, a Frenchman! I trembled with indignation and fury. I ended up shouting that, just as the Maréchal had said, England would have its neck wrung like a chicken! Olivier responded by calling me a fascist. Enough was enough. I bellowed that if he betrayed his Homeland, as well as the wife and daughter whom he was abandoning like a coward, then he was no longer my son. I cursed him. Olivier slammed the door to my office on his way out and found his own way back to the station, without even visiting the cemetery to pay his respects at the tomb of she who had given him life.

That was two years ago. I haven't seen him since. The next day, I merely called to ask Ilse to tell him who was no longer my son that I would keep my promise to arrange a meeting with the official we had spoken about.

*

The Prefect, Roger Langeron, is a dignified man, who has all my respect and good will, and I was sorry to see him arrested (on the basis of a misunderstanding) and replaced. Certainly, the only failing of which one might accuse that humanist is that of having been somewhat half-hearted in his application of the firm measures required by the situation, and called for in dealing with the Jewish leper.

The elite functionary, who at that time had been running the capital's police force for six years and had completely overhauled its functions and methods, adapting them to the changing and growing needs of an ever-evolving Paris – it was he who created the post of officer of the peace, the mobile superintendency and the flying squad of the Judicial Police – received me in his office one morning in September 1940. Behind him, the entire wall was covered by a map of the capital, on which each building was drawn in perspective. We could see the Seine from his window. I explained to Monsieur Langeron that my daughter-in-law, born in 1913 to a respectable, middle-class Berlin family, the Wolffsohns, had married my son in 1934 and assumed French citizenship the following year, pursuant to the 1927 law. And although there was certainly no reason to be, I was concerned – most vaguely, to be sure – by the idea that her file might be subject to review.

Monsieur Langeron's intelligent eyes sparkled behind his delicate glasses, above which sat thick, coal-black eyebrows that almost looked as if they had been drawn with a paintbrush, and a smooth crown, while beneath a straight, equally dark moustache, his thin lips broke into an amiable smile. It suddenly occurred to me that the Prefect rather resembled the actor Groucho Marx, and how amusing it would be if he turned out to be Jewish.

'My dear Monsieur Husson,' he exclaimed with open arms. 'Do you know how many people might be subject to this review?'

I confessed my ignorance.

'About nine hundred thousand! And have you any idea how long it will take the Commission, with its meagre staff, to look into every case?'

The Prefect smiled at me, then sighed.

'Four, five years, I would say ...'[6] Pulling a sheet of paper from a folder lying on his desk, he pointed out certain lines.

'You see, we shall proceed by year, in an order whose logic defies me. The Commission, God knows why, decided to start with 1936, the year of the Popular Front. The years 1939 and 1940 will be next, then 1937 and 1938, followed by 1927 up to 1935, the year that concerns you. So your daughter-in-law's case won't come up until ... 1945, perhaps?'

Bringing the tips of his long, spatulate fingers together, Monsieur Langeron leaned forward.

'Madame Husson wouldn't have anything to hide from us, by any chance? Concerning her religion? I ask because the Commission's main task will be to denaturalise Jews.'

I feigned indignation.

'You know my views, Monsieur le Préfet. You certainly won't find any Yids in my family.'

His face grew sullen at these words. He dryly shut the folder.

'So much the better for you, Monsieur Husson. Because the situation is hardly going to improve for the Israelites. Nonetheless, for the sake of a writer of your stature, and that of your daughter-in-law, who is no doubt a most respectable individual, I am prepared to make her file disappear ... if that is what you wish.' He gave me a probing look. Monsieur Langeron waited, observing me with some interest.

I finally managed to stammer out: 'I would be very grateful if you could, Monsieur le Préfet.'

He nodded his head.

'Fine. You can count on me.'

Monsieur Langeron jotted down Ilse's place and date of birth, as well as her Christian name and surname and those of her parents.

Picking up the telephone receiver, he asked a certain Monsieur Anfray to come and see him in his office. Then the Prefect rose and put a curt end to our interview.

16

That autumn, which saw me lose a son, was otherwise replete with pleasurable compensations.

These were first and foremost political and spiritual. France, having been secularised to the brink of death, had found a new Saviour. While she had felt the dismal and tragic impact of her failures – having forgotten and scorned the ancient French traditions of moral living and family virtues – my Motherland had seen her sins forgiven by God's mercy. After sixty years, she had been delivered from the yoke of radicalism and anti-Catholicism, universal suffrage and parliamentarianism, the malicious and imbecilic domination of schoolteachers ... Military defeat proved to be an opportunity for recovery, a promise of regeneration.

My fellow academician Jacques Chardonne wrote: 'Maréchal Pétain has counselled France wisely. And the most sensible of revolutions has taken place in silence. It is sweet because it is irresistible.'[7] Monsieur Roger Bonnard, Dean of the Bordeaux Law Faculty, declared in *La Revue du Droit public*: 'In our leader, Maréchal Pétain, France now has a guide of incomparable and almost superhuman wisdom and thoughtful command that will prevent her from going astray and lead her along the path of truth.' In *Le Petit Parisien*, I read these judicious words of J.-H. Rosny the Younger, the venerable President of the Académie Goncourt: 'As France sets off behind her leader, Pétain, in a Collaboration that is destined to raise Europe to the greatest heights of her power, it has been most profitable to draw up an inventory of the moral forces at her disposal. Is literature not one of those forces, one of the most powerful tools for ensuring the superiority of any civilisation?' Pierre Taittinger dedicated a book 'To the Maréchal, the new Christ, who has sacrificed himself to redeem a vanquished France'. And to complete that redemption, we were to learn from our conquerors. As early as 1939, the prodigious Céline, the scourge of Israel, had begun urging – in *L'École des cadavres*, which his publisher Robert Denoël had rightly called the application of the Jewish Theory to France, and a prophetic book – a total alliance between Hitler's Germany and France. Bernard Grasset, who had been received by the Maréchal in Vichy in the summer of 1940 and returned to Paris in early August, and who had always been most generous in his encouragement of me, announced that Germany must serve as an example to us. I shared my publisher's national-socialist perspective. We had both long admired your Führer, who understands the importance of publishers and writers, and for whom no political action has meaning unless it serves to frame and underpin a spiritual one.

I joined Eugène Deloncle's brand-new Mouvement Social Révolutionnaire, whose acronym MSR can so neatly be read in French as 'Aime et sers', meaning 'love and serve', and whose founding members included my friends the gifted journalist Jean Fontenoy and General Lavigne-Delville, hero of the Great War, as well as the industrialist Eugène Schueller, owner of L'Oréal and Monsavon. The movement, which is supported by your Ambassador, His Excellency Monsieur Abetz, has adopted the mandate to build a new Europe, in cooperation with National Socialist Germany and all other European nations liberated from liberal capitalism, Judaism, Bolshevism and Freemasonry; to reduce those Jews remaining in France to a lowly status that will prevent them from polluting our race; and to forge a socialist economy that will ensure the fair distribution of wealth by raising salaries and increasing production.

The compensations were creative, too. In Paris, the major publishing houses (other than two that had been owned by Jews and had had to be shut down) went back to work to satisfy the urgent demand of a public hungry for books. Assured of the certainty of being published, I started work on three new projects: an historical novel, *Constance de Saxe*; a four-act play, *Rollo*; and an essay on Saint Aubert, Bishop of Avranches, who built the sanctuary of Mont Saint-Michel after the archangel appeared to him in a dream and said, 'Now is the moment of salvation and strength, and the reign of our Lord and the power of Christ. You will build me a temple here so that the children of this land shall invoke me and I shall come to their aid.' The parallels with the current circumstances were obvious, and I intended to dedicate the essay to the Maréchal, whom all the little children of France had invoked and who had come to their aid.

At the same time, under the enlightened instruction of the Occupier, the Parisian publishing world had been purified by the banning of the works of, among others, the Mann brothers, the psychoanalyst Freud, Zweig, the poet Heine (another Jew), Trotsky, the recent pamphlets of Malraux and, later, Gide – courtesy of the German–Soviet pact – for his *Return from the USSR* (although it is the sole work of merit by that Voltaire of pederasty). These were, in the main, books that had systematically poisoned French public opinion with their mendacity and tendentiousness. Betraying the hospitality that France had extended to them, these political refugees – and the Jews in particular – had, in their writings, pushed tirelessly for a war from which they had shamelessly hoped to profit.

But what mattered most to me was this: I had regained my home, my office, my writing desk; my window overlooking Quai de Verdun, at which, seized by renewed inspiration, I sat and watched the timeless landscape that Rollo,[8] 'Hrolf the Walker', and his Nordic pirates had once gazed upon, voracious and enthralled. In the longboats known as sea serpents, they had sailed the coasts, prowled the river mouths and, in search of a new homeland free from the oppressive rule of Harald Fairhair, ravaged France, burned its cities and pillaged its abbeys. Here the Seine bent in upon itself like the coil of some gigantic snake risen from the depths of time, carving the white cliffs of Vexin, embracing the fertile, silt-rich plain that shimmered in the distance, and upon which men bent themselves in turn.

I reconnected with my work, and with solitude, bolstered by the hills of my Duchy of Normandy, its ancient ruined towers, its sloping pastures and placid, slow-moving livestock; its rich harvests, its trees heavy with apples, plums and cherries, the shade of its hedgerows; the heron circling above the islands, the cormorants playing in the backwaters, and in the vast sky the larks, the gulls and the salt wind wafting in from the sea.

Ilse and Hermione did not come to Andigny that summer.

Olivier left Paris in early October with the aim of crossing the border into Spain.

In mid-autumn I received a call from my daughter-in-law. This was a few days after the Maréchal's meeting with your Führer at which, together, these two great men laid the foundations for a sincere Collaboration at the heart of the new European order. For France, it was the end of its withdrawal from history and the dawn of its revival. Ilse's voice was tense and anxious. She asked if she and the little one could come and spend Saturday and Sunday with me. Nothing could have given me greater pleasure. I awaited them, my heart pounding, on the station platform.

The German descended from the train cautiously. At the villa, my daughter-in-law took off her coat in the front hall and announced that she was pregnant.

I felt as if it was I who was being kicked in the stomach. 'Olivier?' I asked, stupidly.

She shrugged her shoulders. 'Of course Olivier. Who else?'

I apologised for my indiscretion and clumsiness. Then I said, 'Does he know?'

She shook her head, then, clearly exhausted, went to sit in the drawing room.

'He left twenty-eight days ago. I've had no news of him since. He has a good friend, Jacques Duchesne, at the BBC. When Olivier manages to reach England safe and sound, someone is supposed to say over the radio, "And we shall go to Valparaíso". May I listen to your wireless?'

My reaction was violent. 'Listen to dissidents? Me?'

Tears welled in her lovely blue eyes. I bent down and took her by the hand.

'Forgive me, my little one. I didn't mean to hurt you. Yes, I understand. We'll listen together, if you'd like …'

She smiled at me, and her smile erased a good many things. And that, Monsieur le Commandant (you see, I keep nothing from you!), is how I violated a ban that I nevertheless respect, and the wisdom of which I would have been the first to acknowledge.

That evening, on the programme 'The French Speak to the French', there were any number of messages, each more poetic and sibylline than the next, but no one mentioned leaving for Valparaíso.

Shortly after her return to Paris, Ilse took a bad tumble as she was leaving her office at the Opéra, where she had found work thanks to her husband's connections. She was taken to the hospital and almost lost the baby. The doctors put her ankle in plaster and prescribed complete rest until the birth. Someone phoned me. I was able to arrange an ambulance to transport my daughter-in-law to Villa Némésis.

I went to Paris over the weekend to fetch Hermione, and I enrolled her temporarily in our local primary school. I should have preferred placing her with the Sisters of the Sainte-Blandine Institute, who offered better schooling, but Ilse was adamantly opposed and I decided it was best not to upset her in her current condition.

Devoting my days to writing, I did not stop for lunch, but in the evenings I took supper with Ilse and Hermione in my daughter-in-law's bedroom on the second floor.

I had our wireless set installed there.

My daughter-in-law remained on her back, her plastered leg resting on cushions.

One Thursday night in December, as I listened with her – I confess, I had succumbed to the detestable habit – some time after 9.30 p.m. a French voice spoke to us from London: 'And we shall go to Valparaíso ... I repeat: And we shall go to Valparaíso.'

Ilse sat up in bed and wept for joy in my arms.

17

My grandson, Omer Aristide Husson, was born on 19 March 1941 in the unseasonable cold of early spring.

The birth was drawn-out and difficult. I paced away the entire day in my office, unable to write or read a single line, listening to the heart-rending cries that reached me all the way from the floor above, to the harried steps of the servants on the stairs, to the injunctions of the midwife and of Dr Dimey, who was overseeing the event.

I felt as if I myself were the father of the child being born – I experienced all the same anxieties, to say the least. I had alerted the doctor to the fact that, should it come down to the Cornelian dilemma between the life of the mother and that of the child, he must at all costs save my daughter-in-law. At last, towards eleven o'clock in the evening, I heard a rising wail. The cook knocked at my door a few moments later to tell me that it was a boy, that Madame Husson had lost consciousness but that the doctor was certain that both were out of danger. When she closed the door behind her, I got down on my knees, my forehead pressed against the drawer of my desk, and thanked the Lord and Our Lady the Virgin Mary for having spared Ilse. I am ashamed to write it, but old soldier that I am, I wept, and my body trembled uncontrollably.

In the father's absence, and in a political balancing act of which any man would be proud, I chose the names of two great French statesmen: Aristide Briand and Philippe Omer Pétain. The former had bestowed his spiritual patronage on my friend Jean Luchaire's review *Notre Temps*. As to the latter, Ilse begrudged me 'Omer' and positively vetoed 'Philippe'. Omer, a monk at Luxeuil, was sent in the year 637 to re-evangelise the Morini, and founded the abbey of Sithiu, known today as Saint-Omer, where he was buried. A charter dating back to 663 tells us that he lost his sight late in life. Without going into detail, I explained to my daughter-in-law that giving a newborn one of the Maréchal's Christian names was like making an inconvertible pledge of allegiance to the new ideas, and that, seeing as foreigners and 'wogs' had come in for their share of bad press of late, could serve if need be as a defence against anyone who might wish to make trouble for 'recently naturalised citizens in our family'. Ilse blushed at these words, and silently acquiesced. Embarrassed, I added that if his father should be unhappy with any of these names, the boy could always be known within the family simply as 'Aristide', to which his father could hardly object. The German nodded again and gave a little smile, apparently reassured. Then she turned a love-filled gaze upon the cradle, where her miserable tadpole of a son lay wrapped in his swaddling clothes. His red wrinkled face filled me with loathing.

Despite what you might be justified in believing, Monsieur le Commandant, the feeling described above was not born of any kind of jealousy, or resentment at not being the father. The truth is that Aristide, who will soon be a year and a half old, is an extraordinarily ugly child. As with Hermione but worse, it was clear to me that the marks of his heredity had skipped a generation before revealing themselves once more. From the outset, all the most repugnant physical characteristics of the sons of Abraham, as confirmed in the exhibition on 'France and the Jew' at the Palais Berlitz in September last year, seemed to me to have been obtrusively thrown together in that monstrous brat. I recognised in him, with a disgust that you can well imagine, the precise scientific description set out by Professor Montandon: the convex nose; the outsized and protruding lower lip;

the moist, bulging eyes; the curly hair; the large, protuberant ears; the exaggerated facial expressions. In addition, the baby's gestures lacked control, and its muscle tone seemed flabby.[9]

Ten days after my grandson's birth, on 29 March 1941, the Maréchal's government established, under French law and entirely independently of the occupying authorities, the Commissariat-General for Jewish Questions and appointed Xavier Vallat as its director. A prominent veteran of the War of 1914–1918, where he lost a leg and an eye, Vallat was a man of deep-rooted Catholic and nationalistic convictions, determined to eradicate totally Jewish culture from France, like a surgeon wielding his scalpel to remove a deadly tumour sprung from a foreign body.

In an article I wrote on this issue in *Le Journal d'Andigny*, whose columns were open to me, I welcomed all such measures that moved the country forward in the right direction. At the same time, I was grateful, despite myself, that my daughter-in-law, protected by her naturalisation and by the fact that her true race was not publicly known, had not had to register as a Jew at police headquarters, which would certainly have caused her problems in her professional life as France finally and vigorously began to purge its public offices of all Levys, Kahns and Dreyfuses. Firm measures were also being taken against foreign Jews. I read in *La Semaine* that five thousand Polish, Czechoslovakian and Austrian Jews, identified with the help of files prepared by Monsieur André Tulard and his assistants, had been summoned to gathering places set up for the occasion, then arrested and transported by the French gendarmerie to a concentration camp near Orléans that had once been a prison camp and was now refitted for this salutary operation.

But it wasn't all so straightforward.

While the harmful ferment was being eliminated from the public stage, by a strange and cruel twist of fate the very opposite was occurring in my private life. As I tragically lost my loved ones one by one – Jeanne, Marguerite, Olivier, all of good, pure French Catholic stock – the impure elements around me, even here at Andigny, an ancient fiefdom of the Norman heartland, were growing and thriving: Ilse, Hermione, Aristide …

Against my own will, my family and my life were being 'Judaised'. Little by little, a surreptitious leprosy was eating away the fabric of a good French Christian family. The attack was all the more cunning for its recourse to a weapon that had always been difficult to defend against – I am referring to love. Familial love to begin with – because, despite everything, I was somewhat fond of Hermione and would probably end up finding something of worth even in the tadpole – but above all authentic love, the state of 'being in love' described by José Ortega y Gasset: sickness, obsession and mania.

Obstinately, and with the perverse masochism of the hypochondriac who ploughs through medical texts in his determination to confirm even the most minor symptom of the illness he suspects, I went back to the writings of the subtle Spanish philosopher.

When we fall into the state of mental withdrawal and psychic angina we call 'being in love', we are lost. In the early days we can still resist; but when the imbalance between the attention we pay to one woman and that we begrudge to others and to the rest of the universe becomes disproportionate, it is no longer within our power to halt the process.

Attention is the supreme tool of the personality; it is the apparatus that regulates our mental life. If it is paralysed we can no longer enjoy freedom of movement. To save ourselves, we must re-expand our field of consciousness, and to do so we must introduce within it other objects capable of depriving the beloved object of its exclusivity. If, at that moment when the state of being in love reaches its apogee, we were suddenly able to see the beloved object from the normal perspective of our attention, its magic power would evaporate. But if we are to do that, we must be able to focus our attention on something else; in other words, we must rise above our own consciousness, which is totally absorbed in that which we love …

Ortega y Gasset's diagnosis is flawless. Word for word, Monsieur le Commandant, this was *exactly* what had happened to me.

Others, the rest of the universe, France, the war, the National Revolution, my own books and honours had all been reduced with the passing weeks, months and years to a futile and microscopic distraction.

My attention was monopolised by Ilse Husson – by Ilse Wolffsohn, Ilse the Jewess, the lovely blonde Jewess with the charming voice, crystalline laugh, moist lips and slender body; the gorgeous young mother and her languid blue eyes, the mere thought of which set my heart leaping and pounding to the rhythm of a wild stampede. It was no longer within my power to halt the process. My paralysed attention left me with no freedom of movement. Saving myself, expanding my field of consciousness to include anything else besides Ilse, proved beyond my capacity. The magical power of the Jewess, whom I now loved like a fool, an old fool, in a condition that was rising to its apogee, was impervious to any readjustment of perspective. My consciousness was totally *occupied* – even more so, if you will allow me a comparison of dubious taste, than my homeland – by the marvellous and incomparable object of my love.

18.

I interrupted my writing to take lunch; now I take pen in hand to approach the most dreadful part of my confession.

Tonight, after sealing this letter and before delivering it to you at the Hôtel Bellevue, I will telephone Ilse.

And all will be said.

My daughter-in-law returned to Paris in May with little Aristide, leaving Hermione with me to complete the academic year at her primary school. Ilse came back every Friday and went home on Sunday. She had returned to work in the Opéra offices. She spent the month of August with us in Andigny, and so we were all four together until September. We had no news of him who was no longer my son, and I didn't care to think about him.

The war, which we had thought would be brief, had begun to look as if it would be prolonged. For the moment, your Führer had put off his conquest of cunning and obstinate Albion to turn the muscle of his Panzer divisions against the Reds. No more Soviet blackmail! Communism would pay – and we hoped, pay dearly. A tremendous movement was unleashed in Eastern Europe. France would need to watch it with eyes wide open; the scale of the vengeance would help her to understand the enormity of the crime.

Until that moment, the war had been waged by the National Socialist Revolution against the Anglo-American plutocracy. As of that memorable 22 June 1941, it became in addition a war against the egregiously debasing form of civilisation embodied by Bolshevism.

This was a new and glorious chapter in the struggle for the European Federation, a vast community at the core of which France has its own special place and important role to play, if only she can find the resolve to do so. In the choice between Russia and Germany, no vacillation was acceptable. The scales must fall from the eyes of those Frenchmen who remained deluded and lived, like Olivier, in a dream world. England was but a smokescreen for the most infernal enterprise of subversion that had threatened humankind in centuries: the Judeo-Bolshevik conspiracy. Thanks to the clear vision and decisiveness of Chancellor Hitler, a new Western Crusade had been launched against the East.

In July, I received a telephone call from Monsieur du Moulin de Labarthète, the Maréchal's Chief of Staff. A reshuffling of the Cabinet was in the works, under the auspices of Admiral Darlan, and I was being considered for the national Information or Education portfolio. Dumbfounded and overwhelmed, I declined the offer – the honour was too great and my abilities too limited. I excused myself on the grounds that I was a writer and not a politician. But the real reason for my refusal was that I had no wish to give up – by dint of having to move to Vichy, and all the travelling and glad-handing that would have been required in my new ministerial capacity – my summer with Ilse, our frequent times together in Andigny, or our excursions in Paris.

This was a new routine that we had inaugurated on 2 July, on the occasion of a charity gala thrown at the Opéra for the benefit of our naval prisoners of war, and for which, because of her job in the administrative offices, my daughter-in-law had been offered two tickets. Serge Lifar and Solange Schwarz were starring in the ballet *Le Chevalier et la Damoiselle* by Philippe Gaubert. Ministers Scapini and de Brinon – my distinguished colleagues on the Franco-German Committee – were in attendance, and Admiral Darlan presided over the proceedings. The stage was a whirlwind of jousting and enchanting costumes. Ilse and I thrilled to the clash of lances, and when the maiden

in white ermine gave her colours to the knight and prayed for him ...
In the interval, Monsieur Rouché, the Director of the Palais Garnier,
was very pleased to meet the famous father-in-law of his secretary,
while Monsieur de Brinon appeared to be in thrall to Ilse. He told her
that she resembled an actress he used to see in the movies. An SS officer
who also happened to be a film buff said that he was probably thinking
of Elsie Berger. My daughter-in-law shivered but kept her composure.
She had often been teased over the resemblance, she quipped with a
laugh.

Of course, Ilse had no idea that *I already knew* about her race.
Monsieur de Brinon lamented Elsie's absence from recent productions.
The officer cackled: '*Jüdin*.[10] We sorted her out ...' The critic Alain
Laubreaux cried 'Bravo!' I glanced over at my companion, who had
gone quite ashen.

I never spoke to her again about the incident, and on our later outings
I was careful to minimise the amount of time spent in the company of
her compatriots, who might count other film enthusiasts in their midst.
She was moved by my discretion, and seemed to be troubled, surprised
and comforted by the fact that the German officer's comment – which
I could not have helped but overhear – had not changed my attitude
towards her. It seemed to have had the effect of increasing the affection
in which my daughter-in-law had long held me.

I took her to the cinema. We saw *La Vierge folle*, a new adaptation
of the play by Henry Bataille. The actor Victor Francen played the
lawyer Amaury, and Annie Ducaux his wife. I could not fail to be
touched by the plot, about a middle-aged man having a secret affair
with a boarding-school girl he had met by chance on a train. As we left
the cinema, I thought that Ilse, too, seemed moved.

The Prix Goncourt for 1941 was awarded to Henri Pourrat, the
candidate I had endorsed. While he was already a writer of some

renown, his latest book, expressing some of the loftiest and most noble French values, provided welcome reassurance to an unsettled public, and strengthened people's support for all the great plans of our Head of State, whom they would stand behind rightly and properly as he worked for the greatest good and honour of my Motherland. I regretted that Francis Carco, Jean Ajalbert and Lucien Descaves had dissented from the majority opinion and had chosen to award an ill-considered 'Free Zone Goncourt' to their nominee, Guy des Cars.

The young Sonderführer Gerhard Heller, from the Propaganda-staffel, a friend to many writers and intellectuals in the Occupied Zone, accompanied me to a meeting with your Ambassador, His Excellency Monsieur Otto Abetz, whom I had known since the early days of the Franco-German Committee when, introduced by Henry de Montherlant, he came to give us a lecture on the Hitler Youth. This remarkable man – a confidant of Ribbentrop's and an adviser to the Chancellor – is courtly, attractive, quite young for such a posting, and has the typically Aryan physique of a magnificent Nordic warrior that I find quite striking. He easily convinced me of the sincerity of his desire for a genuine and fruitful cultural collaboration, in addition to the political one, between our two great peoples. From that moment on, Monsieur Abetz regularly invited me to the receptions held by the German Institute, whose abundant buffets were particularly appreciated by Parisian writers reduced to rationing, which has had little effect on me, enjoying as I do – and as you do, too – special relations with the farmers of the Andigny district. Shortly thereafter, I had the honour that autumn of participating in the first great official delegation of French writers to Weimar, in the excellent company of Marcel Jouhandeau, Drieu la Rochelle, Brasillach, Abel Bonnard and Ramon Fernandez. André Fraigneau represented my publishing house. Jean Giono had also been invited, but had begged off on the pretext that he had been denied the use of a chauffeur and car that he had requested for the trip. The ever-obliging Lieutenant Heller introduced us to the distinguished authors of your country, and Arno Breker – a committed Francophile who, as a young sculptor, had lived in an attic room on the Avenue d'Orléans during his time in Paris – threw us a party at his studio in Jäckelsbruck surrounded by his monumental works. The climax of our visit was a solemn ceremony held in the presence of Dr Goebbels.

But I must confess that the most moving moment of my visit to your country was when, thanks to Sonderführer Heller, who had conveyed my request to the Reich Ministry of Propaganda, I was able to attend, alone in a vast theatre furnished with upholstered seats, screenings of two films: *Das Flötenkonzert von Sans-souci* and *Der Kongress tanzt*, both featuring Elsie Berger. I knew every film in which she had appeared, thanks to the complete list contained in the report provided by the Dardanne Agency, and I had scrupulously noted their titles before my departure.

19

The general population had no great love for the Jews but had tolerated them thus far. French tradesmen, in particular, would have been glad to be rid of the Yids by reason of the underhand nature of their competition. And many doctors sent letters to the Medical Association alerting it to colleagues with names of dubious origin, so that the association might inform the Gestapo of foreigners of irregular status, who were speedily investigated. I can affirm that the anti-Jewish measures undertaken by the German authorities and my government elicited no protest from the vast majority. There was just a trickle of complaints, emanating from a minority of the overly charitable who felt that our articles in the press were too vindictive, and could therefore lead to such excesses as attacks on synagogues and the like. And yet, when Paul Riche wrote in *Au Pilori*, 'The Jew is not a man. He is a stinking beast. We rid ourselves of lice. We fight epidemics. We put down microbial invasions. We defend ourselves against sickness and death – and thus, against the Jews,' well, I can assure you, Monsieur le Commandant, that deep down most Frenchmen thought exactly the same!

In February, the occupying forces issued a regulation forbidding kikes to leave their homes between 8 p.m. and 6 a.m. or to change their primary residence, under pain of imprisonment, fine or internment in a camp for hooknoses. I approved – the Jewish problem concerns all Jews; this was an issue of *race* and not merely of religion. Sadly, the tribal headmen are already safe in London and New York, where they pursue their baleful business. For the remainder, those still within our grasp, *all must meet the same fate!*

Let none talk of formal justice, for this is a matter of public health. France is a convalescent, and her conqueror sits at her bedside pointing the way to salvation, which calls first and foremost for the excision of the Semitic cancer within. The Jewish influence on a country's affairs saps its aspirations to greatness and its capacity to preserve its moral patrimony. In the occupied territories, the German authorities have devised ways to subject the Jews residing therein to strict monitoring in order to maintain total control over their activities. Our Kings of France long ago shared the same aim. Philippe-Auguste issued a decree in 1206 – that is, I note in passing, just a few years after the construction of the stronghold that looms above our city of Andigny – that Jews must wear a wheel badge. Shortly thereafter, Pope Innocent III prohibited Jews from dressing like Christians. Later in the Middle Ages, the wheel was replaced by a brightly coloured and grotesquely misshapen cowl. In England in 1434, King Henry VI ordered the children of Abraham to wear a yellow circular patch sewn onto their outer clothing. Such edicts are so numerous that I could hardly list them all.

I mention these few only to point out that three months ago, when they first compelled the Jews of the Occupied Zone to wear a distinctive sign – as they already had in Germany, Poland, Luxembourg, Belgium and the Netherlands – the occupying authorities were merely conforming to a very ancient and very sage tradition; and it is my hope, for the reasons explained above, that the government of the Maréchal shall soon follow suit in the Southern Zone.

I must also confess that all the recent measures that I have just enumerated had only confirmed me in the belief that my daughter-in-law had acted wisely in marrying my son and then applying for French citizenship. Ilse thereby avoided the indignities of a situation that would have quickly become unbearable: prohibitions against owning a wireless set or a telephone, using a telephone booth, attending public entertainments, and so on and so forth. I should have been forced to request a dispensation for her, via the intermediary of Monsieur de Brinon, whose wife, née Franck, is Jewish and, as the spouse of Vichy's Ambassador to Paris, is naturally exempt from having to wear the star. But while I am confident of the friendship and good will of that excellent man, I have been told that the Gestapo grants such extremely rare exemptions only to the wives of members of the Maréchal's inner circle.

As these regulations, which I had long dearly sought, gradually came into force in my country, I was gripped by an ever more compelling anxiety; each new dictate represented another threat to the one being who held any importance for me, the woman towards whom all my thoughts continually gravitated and in whom was concentrated the despairing love that constricted my heart.

One day in early June as I watched Ilse dandle little Aristide in her arms, it occurred to me that the most powerful shield for deflecting any suspicion of Jewishness concerning her was, paradoxically, my notorious hatred for Jews. Taking the appalling schizophrenia that was tearing me apart to its logical extreme, I therefore spent several hours in my office wielding my most mordant and vengeful pen to compose an article for *Le Journal d'Andigny* that I felt most likely to repel the dark gaze of suspicion from my family once and for all.

The time has come!

As of Sunday 7 June, all Jews six years and older will have to wear the Jewish star, the Star of David, clearly visible on the left side of the chest. From now on , we will be able to see who we are dealing with. From now on, Levy, Blum and Cohen, even if they call themselves Dubois, Dupont and Durand, will be powerless to abuse our trust and good faith.

The six-pointed star will identify them at first sight,

and only those who close their eyes will be deceived – the Judaised and the incurable imbeciles who pity the fate of the eternally persecuted 'poor Jews'.

Let there be no doubt, the Jews are merely TOLERATED – and that, on a provisional basis. That is what every French national of sound mind must firmly believe. We have given them the right of asylum, nothing more. Our affairs no longer concern them. It is up to us to ensure that they stop meddling in them once and for all. And when the time comes to determine their fate, they must have no say in the matter.

If Vichy is truly sincere that there should not be two Frances, divided by the Jewish question – and on this point we have no doubts about the resolve and good will of the Head of State – the Jews, all Jews, those on the far side of the line as well as those on this, must henceforth wear the distinguishing star. When that happens, a real change will have come into effect, and we will be convinced that the National Revolution is finally on the march.

What we have accomplished against those scoundrels to date essentially counts for nothing. The few timid decrees printed in *Le Journal officiel* have barely been implemented. The yellow star may make certain Catholics blanch, but it is in keeping with the strictly Christian tradition of the wheel.

A politician once said: 'If the Jews were black or blue, there would be no Jewish question because everyone would be able to recognise and avoid them.' The yellow star will correct the quirk of nature that has made the one human race that is radically opposed to the others difficult to distinguish from them.

Let us pay no heed to the hypocrisy of the moderates,

the mediocre and the neutrals! The Maréchal has a powerful dictum, quoted just days ago by Robert Brasillach: 'Life is not neutral.' It would be truly dangerous for the Jews to remain mixed in with Aryans and able to pass for them.

The wearing of the star of Zion will henceforth prevent all subterfuge. It will topple the edifice, carefully built up over the past century and a half, of Jewish anonymity. This new dispensation will finally protect the French people from the pernicious influence of those who, with no hereditary right, have for too long ruled the roost in our country, and who are today the born enemies of the new European Order in which France must look to herself to carve out a worthy place.

We must protect the race!

And to that end, let us shout it loud and clear:

Death to the Jew! Death to Jewish treachery, duplicity and cunning! Death to Jewish influence! Death to Jewish usury! Death to Jewish demagoguery! Death to all that is false, ugly, dirty, repugnant, negroid, crossbred, Jewish! This is the last recourse of the white man hunted, robbed, flayed and murdered by the Semites, and who has now summoned the strength to free himself of the abominable yoke!

Death! Death to the Jew! Yes. Say it again! Repeat after me: Death! D.E.A.T.H. to the Jew!

So there!

With bitter satisfaction, thinking of the Jewess whom I loved madly and wanted to save more than myself, I signed – just as later this evening I shall sign this letter to you, Monsieur le Commandant – I signed with great sweeping strokes of my pen, 'PAUL-JEAN HUSSON'.

20

My faithful Rochet-Schneider gave up the ghost last May, on my return from Rouen where I had attended a meeting chaired by Jacques Doriot. With Lieutenant Heller's assistance, I acquired a Belgian Imperia TA-11 Jupiter saloon, a model which owes its elegant lines (unfortunately blemished by an unsightly gas generator) to the talents of the French designer Chadefeau, and which was originally equipped with one of your powerful four-cylinder Adler engines.

I finished my essay on the Bishop of Avranches, which I intended to dedicate to the Maréchal. I suggested to Ilse, who had joined us in Andigny with Aristide on the night of 12 June, that we take a trip to Mont Saint-Michel. Besides giving me the opportunity to show the German and her children one of the marvels of the Christian world, the outing would let me assess the performance of my new automobile. Moreover, on the night of 29–30 May, another Anglo-American air raid had done cruel damage to a Paris suburb. The toll included some fifty dead, more than a hundred wounded, and two hundred homes destroyed. I preferred that my family spend as much time as possible in Normandy, where everything was calm. We left at dawn on Saturday the 13th, in weather that was every bit as glorious as it had been that day in June, during the exodus.

Things happen at Mont Saint-Michel that one sees nowhere else. Just consider the miracle of Saint Aubert – in the middle of the night, a dazzling light envelops the monastery. Lightning or firebrands, Pentecost or Apocalypse, it is a sign from on high. The Bishop of

Avranches sees the blaze, calls for his horse to be saddled, heads straight for the abbey at full gallop, tears off his purple vestments and becomes a monk. The story captures the very essence of the Mount's holy spirit.

There are days when I envy the man who has entered the priesthood. Has he not received the Holy Spirit? Is he not *a man of the Holy Spirit*? The Book of Revelation tells us of a woman (the Church) clothed with the sun; but is not a priest or a monk clothed with joy, clothed with love, clothed with light, clothed with the sun? Every little bird has something to sing about the glory of God. The priest has the great privilege of giving voice every Sunday, every day, to that which the over-brimming heart, all-capacious as it is, is too small to contain. What sweetness merely to speak out loud the name of Our Lord and his Holy Mother! It is what the psalm calls *super mel ori meo*. The honey at the tip of his staff that caused Jonathan to swoon.

Alas, in truth I am of little worth in comparison to that man of the Holy Spirit – I who trifle at weaving sentences and rhyming fragments, and whom the presence at my side of one woman among them all, the presence of her fragile and mortal flesh beside me in the Imperia hurtling towards the sea, causes to swoon!

We took lunch in Avranches, majestically perched on its high, gently sloping hilltop, exposed to the sea winds and invasions, conquered and reconquered by the dukes of Normandy and Brittany, the kings of France and England, yet somehow managing to retain its primal episcopal solemnity. Having eaten, we took a short stroll along the walkway at the botanic garden, lined with age-old elms and overlooking one of the most beautiful landscapes of France. The valley of the Sée and the Sélune is a great ocean of luxuriant green, while in the distance the yellowish strands outline the curve of a crescent gulf, ending in the two headlands at Granville and Pontorson.

In the middle of the gulf, like some fantasy castle, Mont Saint-Michel rose on a spindly black outcrop. Seen from a distance, veiled in fog and as if lost at sea, it looked more like a colossal menhir than a human construction. Its triangular form clearly radiated the three powers united in the All: man, nature and God. This threefold communion – which decadent Surrealists like Breton and Man Ray seek in life's occult horrors, or in some nonsense about immersion in primary sources – is manifest unequivocally and with unparalleled nobility in the Mount. Standing there, the rock is the unmoving arbiter, the scornful judge of the restless world. On the slopes of the inspired hill, only prayer rises to assault the sky.

We resumed our travels in the direction of Pontorson, then drove along the coast. Low farmhouses still bordered the road, but gradually the trees began to thin out, giving way to the paludal vegetation of samphire marshes. We were coming to the expanse of dunes and sand that extend, gleaming like a sallow mirror, all the way to the open sea. I stopped the car and we walked along the beach as the tide ebbed. Leaning on Ilse's shoulder as I pointed to the imposing scenery, I quoted Flaubert at the top of my lungs:

> The empty horizon stretches on, spreads out, and finally dissolves its chalky terrain in the yellow of the strand. The ground becomes firmer, you begin to smell salt in the air. It feels like a desert from which the sea has withdrawn … The waves are far off, so distant that they can no longer be seen; it is not their roar one hears but some sort of vague, elusive, air-borne murmur, like the voice of solitude itself, which may be nothing but the dizzying silence …

As we approached the Mount, the individual buildings and structures took shape, forming a uniquely strange and imposing ensemble, a living relic bequeathed to the people of our century by their very Christian brothers of the Middle Ages – one that elicited awe-struck exclamations from Hermione. My daughter-in-law, carrying little Aristide in her arms, seemed to be deeply impressed as well. We walked along the causeway, alongside which the fishermen moor their boats, and which ends at the solid wall of the 'Avancée', the exterior defensive works of the holy site. My attention was suddenly drawn to a little girl of about twelve years old, a wild child digging for cockles in the sand and singing an ancient and simple melody that I had never heard before. I consigned the words to memory and wrote them down that night at the inn.

Handsome bargee, barge along,
Long live love!
Teach me to sing,
Long live the bargee!

Come aboard my boat,
Long live love!
I will teach you,
Long live the bargee!

When the maiden came aboard,
Long live love!
She began a-crying,
Long live the bargee!

What is it, maiden?
Long live love!
Wherefore do you cry?
Long live the bargee!

If there were other verses, the child didn't know them, because she kept returning to the first quatrain and repeating herself. Ilse listened, like me, and when our glances met it seemed to me that my daughter-in-law blushed slightly.

Then we reached the granite foundation of the holy Mount itself.

We passed through the King's Gate. Above our heads, a stone lion rested his paw on the abbatial crest, upon which salmon swam against a wavy background. We began to climb the one street that zigzags along the flank of the Mount, leading to the abbey by ramped stairs. We passed a small group of German officers, no doubt on leave, as they descended, having completed their visit. They smiled at the children and their mother. Two hours after we had begun our ascent, the tide was beating against the Avancée rampart, and soon the encircling waves had turned the isolated Mount into an island.

Over dinner at the inn, I thought Ilse looked preoccupied and sad. I imagined that she was missing Olivier, that his absence became all the more bitter on family outings of which he ought to have been part. Hermione and I were more chatty; I told my granddaughter, whose brown eyes gleamed with excitement, stories of the glorious past of Mont Saint-Michel and the life of Saint Aubert. The child was top of her class at school. Will she one day be as clever as my lost Jeanne?

We were given a large room with two big twin beds and a small side room where Hermione and Aristide would share a more modest bed – my granddaughter loved playing mother, and the birth of her little brother had delivered a real live baby doll. The children, tired out by the drive and the visit to the abbey, immediately fell asleep, curled up together like in Boilly's painting, *Amour familial*. I washed, then went to lie in the bed next to Ilse's. I was – almost – as close to her as I had been during our forced stay in Rânes, in the shed behind the café.

I was about to turn off the light when my companion suddenly began to speak in a flat voice.

'Last Tuesday in Paris, I saw and heard something that I found very painful. I can't get it out of my head.'

'So tell me, my child. I'm listening,' I answered.

'It was on the métro. By chance, I happened to get in the last carriage. You know that it's been ruled that Jews are only allowed in the last carriage?'

'Yes, I've heard that.'

'You approve of it, obviously. You don't consider what it might actually mean. Anyway, that Tuesday afternoon, there was only one passenger in that last carriage wearing a yellow star. I watched her run to catch the train, at the station after École Militaire. A young woman, maybe twenty years old. A student, I think. Clearly someone from a good family, well but plainly dressed. She looked intelligent and honest. Rather pretty. She stood panting, very pale. I watched her from the corner of my eye. There was something appealing about her, this French student. I noticed that she had tears in her eyes. Staring straight ahead of her, the girl was biting her lip to stop herself from crying in public.'

Ilse bit her own lip. Then, with some effort, she went on.

'A few stations on, just as the young student with the yellow star was about to get off, a lady in the carriage spoke to her. In a friendly voice, and loud enough so that most of the other passengers could hear, she said, "Hello, Mademoiselle."'

I watched Ilse closely. Her eyes misted over. She fell silent. I asked, 'Is that all?'

My daughter-in-law glared at me. 'Isn't that enough?'

'The world is at war, my dear. France is occupied. Some people are responsible for this state of affairs, and now steps are being taken. Everything will be better soon, you'll see.'

Ilse shook her head, repeating in a rising voice: 'Better? Better? What you really mean is that things will be better when the police send that student I saw to some camp in the East.'

'Not necessarily. No one will send her east if she's French.'

'Paul-Jean, didn't you yourself write in *Au Pilori* – don't deny it, someone showed it to me and I read it – "The yellow star has unmasked a few Jews. We still have to count them all, denounce them and kick them out of Europe. They must be prevented from doing further harm." *Doing further harm*? That student I saw in the Paris métro on Tuesday, with her textbooks and notebooks, what's harmful about her? *What harm has she done?*'

I found it difficult to respond, because the violent emotions overwhelming the woman I loved communicated themselves to me and threw me off balance. I mumbled something or other, and Ilse forged ahead.

'I could feel what she was feeling. I could put myself in her shoes. I knew that for the past two days, the eyes of *every single person* she had met had immediately been drawn to that star, to her chest. Everyone: family, friends, perfect strangers. And no matter how they reacted, the first thing they saw was the star. That star burning into her chest. There were tears of pain and revulsion in her eyes. She struggled to maintain her dignity so that people could see what dignity looks like. She did the most courageous thing of all. It takes more courage to wear the star out in the open than to hide!'

She buried her head in her hands. I looked on, horrified and despairing. 'My little one,' I whispered.

'The way people looked at her,' she went on, less vehemently but with her face still hidden behind her hands. '*Everyone*. Some looked surprised. Curious. Mocking. Severe. Hostile. Evasive. Scornful. Blank. Moved. Shocked. Compassionate. And it's those compassionate looks, and the friendly smiles, that hurt the most.'

I rose from my bed, crossed over to hers and put my right arm around her shoulder. I could feel her sobs more than I could hear them. I caressed her skin beneath the thin fabric of her nightgown. Ilse sniffled, shaking her head.

'I saw this kind of thing in Germany. I never thought I'd see it here. I thought this was the country of liberty. My countrymen did this to you, but the fact is you were ripe for it. You know, this France of yours disgusts me!'

'You've met some charitable Frenchmen, too. That lady …'

I hardly knew what I was saying.

Ilse wept like a child.

I thought I heard her say, 'I'm afraid … I'm afraid …'

Deeply moved, I stroked her hair and whispered in her ear.

'You're not alone. Be strong, little one. I know everything, I understand you. I'm watching over you. I'll protect you. My dear little Ilse. Don't be afraid, I'll protect you, my Ilse, my little Dorte …'

She pulled away from me forcefully. Her blue eyes stared at me, incredulous and suspicious.

'What did you say? What did you call me? *Nobody* knows that nickname!'

I stuttered that it had been Franz, as he was leaving on the night of the wedding, who had asked me to protect his sister. I recalled his words:

Monsieur Husson, I am entrusting Dorte to you. So that through you – a war hero, a member of the Academy, and a great poet – and through all you represent, the spirit of Eternal France may watch over her!

I knew that her brother was dead; my daughter-in-law didn't. But completely overcome by his words, she took refuge in my arms, whispering, '*Oh, Franz! Franz, mein lieber Franz* …' I tasted the salt of her tears on my lips. I felt the heat of her trembling body, I felt her hair brush against my skin, I felt our hearts beat in double rhythm. And Ilse, without doubt, felt the hardness of my member against her nightshirt. She did not push me away. I embraced her, Monsieur le Commandant, as I had never embraced a woman before. That night, I know, she came to understand the full power of my love for her. Soon, she was nothing but sighs and flutters, caress built upon caress, and we climaxed at the same time, two great intermingled cries that half woke the little girl in the room next door.

21.

Ilse woke up before I did. When I opened my eyes, she was leaving the room with the little ones, on her way down to the breakfast room.

On the return journey – all the way to Paris, where I had business to attend to – my daughter-in-law barely unclenched her teeth.

Her most coherent statement was to the effect that, with the academic year coming to an end, she had decided to pull Hermione out of school immediately, and that the child would stay with her in Paris. I did not protest, but the decision saddened me. We stopped at the villa to pick up the little girl's things.

As I drove, I pondered the reasons for her hostile attitude. Did Ilse regret her night of abandon? Did she think I had trapped her into it? That I was, in the final analysis, a reprobate who could not even be trusted with a little girl? Was she thinking of Olivier and feeling remorseful? All of that would have been natural and plausible. But was Ilse also afraid that, in the panic brought on by her anxieties and terror, she had said too much about the Jews of the Occupied Zone and the yellow star to a kike-hater like her father-in-law?

And yet, I had done my best to reassure her. It had even been my promise of protection that, alongside the recollection of her brother, had thrown her into my arms.

In any case, I was uncertain how to deal with the unexpected change in our relationship that our night together had precipitated. My love, now more intense than ever, was tinged with embarrassment and fear. What would happen when Olivier returned to France at the end of the war? Would his wife and I be able to look him in the eye?

Above all, would that which had come to pass in the inn on Mont Saint-Michel recur soon? Or ever again? How would my daughter-in-law behave on her next visit to Andigny? And should I, one way or another, suggest that she join me in my room? Or would I be expected to join her in hers?

Ilse provided me with an answer of sorts upon our arrival at Rue Richer by jumping out of the car, grabbing her bags and her children and vanishing into the courtyard without inviting me up for a cup of tea or a nightcap, as she usually did.

I took refreshment on a café terrace on the Boulevards, strolled through the neighbourhood – where I noticed the abundance of yellow stars – and went for dinner with Ramon Fernandez on Rue Saint-Benoît, in the company also of Drieu la Rochelle and Sonderführer Heller, before returning to Normandy that same night, in grim humour and even more heavy-hearted than I had been before our travels.

Having decided to let time do its work and to wait for my daughter-in-law to come round, and too distraught to return to high-minded authorship, I devoted myself to simple journalistic projects that, whilst allowing me to express my unvarnished opinions, served incidentally to continue shielding my family from suspicion. I wrote a second article for *Le Journal d'Andigny* along the lines of the first. I reproduce this piece below – you read it at the time of its publication, for I recall your complimenting me on it, as did Dr Hild – in order to prove, if proof were needed, that whilst I may have been harbouring a Jewess within my family, for reasons well known to you, I also never hesitated to publicly denounce the Jewish threat. I entitled the article 'Andigny Must Set an Example!'

> What great things have the Aryans produced? They have given the world the concept of the State, the law, public

administration, the arts, science, philosophy, poetry. In short, the very essence of what we call civilisation.

And the others?

To the Arabs we owe numbers, to the Chinese, the compass.

And to the Jews?

The black market!

As of Sunday 7 June of this year, the Jews of the Occupied Zone have finally been compelled to wear the yellow star. In the capital – whither I go at least once a week, if only to attend the meetings of the Academy, whose work on the Dictionary has been regrettably delayed by the fact that so many of our colleagues remain in the Southern Zone – the abundance of Jews on the streets has opened the eyes of even the blindest among us. My Sunday stroll yesterday was surprising and shocking. Especially on the Boulevards where the stars began to come out in the early afternoon. Alone or in little groups, our Hebes strolled along, all walking in the same direction – westward, towards the Champs-Élysées. Their numbers swelled by the minute. There are swarms of them! They are a veritable multitude, which the real Parisian can only gaze upon in amazement.

But what has this to do with our pleasant little town, where the only stars one sees, at the weekend or during the summer, are worn by a few fortunate owners of second homes?

My work on the Town Council has allowed me to learn that we have among us a certain Amédée Lévy, who has been appointed as the official caretaker of the town cemetery. He is 100 per cent Jewish, a childless widower with no military record who has never appeared on any list qualifying him for employment in a reserved occupation. He was given the job even though French veterans wounded in the Great War – of whom I am one myself – have been left to moulder on those selfsame lists.

How is it, moreover, that this person should have been sworn in even before he had been naturalised? His naturalisation, too, could well be ascribed to certain connections within the former republican regime. In any case, his presence on the public rolls is highly suspect. His insolent swagger is a disgusting challenge. He has been summoned to the town hall on several occasions because of his status as a Jew, but the man, cunning like all of his race, has always 'fallen on his feet'.

By dint of what secret influence?

Amédée Lévy managed to obtain a veteran's certificate, no doubt fraudulently, but he has been stripped of it. In the meantime, his case cannot drag on forever. This individual's file must be fat with surprises. The police or the gendarmerie would be well advised to look into it!

That is why I demand that a thorough investigation be launched of this person, who is occupying a public post that is not his by right. We need to know now by what authority he is exempt, as he claims to be, from having to wear the Jewish insignia.

I find it alarming that exceptions are made for every bit of scum that has washed up on our shores from foreign ghettos since the days of the Popular Front. Enough is enough – people will tolerate this no more! And yet the solution to the 'Jewish problem' is simple. Until they can be sterilised or exterminated, the Jews should all be sent to labour camps. Real Frenchmen wish to see the Jews stooped over French soil, mattock in hand.

Let us rid the cities of France of their Jews! Our sub-prefecture has given refuge to one single Jew. Kick him out!

In setting such an example of public health policy, Andigny would become the first town in France without a single Jew!

I signed it: 'Paul-Jean Husson, member of the Académie Française, Officer of the Légion d'Honneur, veteran of 1914–1918, decorated for bravery, war-wounded, Collaboration Group registration No. 50-144-H, literary section.'

Having had no news from Rue Richer in ten days, I called. The phone rang for an unusually long time, and then Hermione answered. We exchanged a few words, and the child told me that her mother had a migraine and couldn't speak to me. I said that I wished her a speedy recovery and that I would call again the following day.

Jittery and anxious, I couldn't bring myself to do it, but called back two days later. Hermione again answered the phone, and informed me that her mother was out. But I briefly thought that I heard Ilse's voice in the background.

I lost heart, and did not call again for several weeks. Happening to pass by Rue du Buet, where Amédée Lévy, the cemetery caretaker, lived, I noticed that the shutters were closed and that the brick walls were covered in graffiti, written in forceful vernacular, strongly encouraging our Yid to pack his bags for Palestine if, among other unpleasant options, he did not want to find himself 'in the oven'. Tickled by the eloquence of certain colourful expressions, I wrote them down with the idea of reusing them in my reportage. I had the opportunity of doing so in July, when a mass round-up of foreign Jews, first housed at the Vélodrome d'Hiver and later in the camp at Drancy

– ultimately to be transferred to the labour camps in the East – proved that our French police had finally decided to take serious measures.

July passed without any contact between me and my family in Paris. I was also concerned for their health, as I knew that the material circumstances of city-dwellers were in continual decline. Food was growing scarce, disappearing off the shelves. Artichokes and tomatoes were now available only with ration tickets. At dawn, hours before the shops opened, women gathered in long queues on the streets, monitored by police officers, in the hope of obtaining a bit of salad or a pound of rotten fruit. As for me out in the country, living quite well on the generosity of our farmers, I vegetated, my heart stricken, wounded, plunged into an abyss of confusion and sorrow. I understood that I would have to give up on Ilse; that our wonderful night would never be repeated; that in burning my bridges I had unwittingly cut myself off from my love for good and all; and that the Lord had judged me severely for the sin of having lain with my son's wife and, worse yet, a Jewess.

On 5 August came the attack in the Jean-Bouin stadium. Hidden behind a hedge like cowards, three men hurled grenades at a group of some fifty German soldiers who had been training on the track. Eight were killed and thirteen wounded, and the criminals escaped.[11] All that morning, I was told, soldiers patrolled the streets, sub-machine guns at the ready, arresting passers-by at random. In reprisal, General Oberg, your Higher SS and Police Leader, had eighty-eight hostages shot, only eighteen foreigners among them. Many of the French citizens sacrificed that morning on Mont Valérien had committed no direct action against the occupying forces, and had been jailed on minor offences. I was deeply upset at the thought that a bunch of Bolsheviks, Jews and Gaullists had caused innocent French blood to be spilled once again, and that the policy of Collaboration between our two great peoples was again under threat because of an act of abject terrorism.

On 19 August, the Anglo-Americans attempted a landing at Dieppe. Your Wehrmacht easily repulsed them after a few hours of fighting. But this sharp clash gave us a good idea of what to expect if France's 'liberators' managed to gain a foothold on terra firma. Our territory would become a battlefield, our cities and villages reduced to ashes, our monuments razed, our population decimated. Two days later, Monsieur de Brinon sent a telegram of thanks to Marshal von Runstedt on behalf of Maréchal Pétain, congratulating him on having so quickly foiled the enemy's advance.

A few days later, during the afternoon of the 27th, I heard the rumble of an engine and then the crunching of gravel on my drive. It was a very hot and lovely day. Although Monsieur de Brinon had invited me, I had not attended the high Mass at Notre Dame, followed by the military parade at Les Invalides in celebration of Legion Day, on the occasion of the first anniversary of the departure of our first contingent of volunteers to the Eastern Front. I went down in my shirtsleeves, having been upstairs writing in my office. The gardener had left the main gate open, and a black Citroën saloon had taken the opportunity to pull up willy-nilly at my front door. Two strangers, both in hat and trench coat despite the heat, were standing beside the car and gazing up at the villa's gables. I went out. One of the men asked to speak to Monsieur Husson.

They looked like policemen, and I thought they might be on the trail of my son. I told them that Olivier was abroad. The one who had spoken first corrected me. 'No, we're looking for Paul-Jean Husson.'

'That's me.'

He took out his card and showed it to me. He belonged to the national police force, there was no mistaking it. I ushered the two officers into my drawing room.

The first introduced himself and his colleague.

'Deputy Chief Inspector Sadorski. And Special Detective Cuvelier. General Inquiries,[12] Third Brigade.'

They sat. I asked the maid to bring them something to drink. I joined them in a cognac – I felt the need for one, because something told me that the visit boded no good.

We drank in silence. Special Detective Cuvelier seemed fascinated by the Boilly painting, the intertwined group portrait *Amour familial*.

'We're here to take custody of the Jew Lévy, the cemetery caretaker,' Deputy Chief Inspector Sadorski explained to me. 'You see, the Feldgendarmes picked him up at home at dawn, and it's our job to take him to jail in Paris. I had a look at his file, and saw the article you wrote in it. Bravo, and congratulations. Without it, the chicken would have flown the coop. The Yid's in for it now!'

I heaved a sigh of relief. The police, it seemed, were only interested in my denunciation. They had come, no doubt, to take my testimony.

'We were told that you spend your time in town these days,' the inspector went on. 'So this is a lucky break. Your name is not unknown to me, as it happens.'

Assuming that the officer had heard of my work, I asked him if he had read any of my books. He seemed amused.

'No, I don't have time to read. You can't imagine how much work we have to do. My group specialises in bagging Jews.'

I was unfamiliar with the expression; Inspector Sadorski explained it to me.

'Our section is on the "public areas" beat, assigned to non-terrorist Jews and foreigners. We have about fifteen detectives. We sometimes get a hand from the youngsters in the PPF,[13] sometimes from the IV-J Division of the Gestapo security service. We mostly work the railway stations and public places. For instance, yesterday at the Gare d'Austerlitz, I see two young girls about to board a train, carrying little suitcases. Look like Jew girls to me … I can tell them straight off. I have a good eye for it. Names I might forget, but faces, never. And even those who don't look Jewish, I *know* they're Jews. I'm wrong once in a thousand times. Me and my colleague, we ask for their papers. They're sisters; they hand us their identity cards, which I'm surprised to find are not marked "Jewess". But their foreign surname looked kikey to me, even if their first names were as French as they come. I ask for their parents' Christian names. The older one answers quick as you like, "Bernard and Pauline". We search their bags, nothing suspicious, just clothes.'

'And underwear,' Detective Cuvelier chimed in with a sly smile.

'Shut up, we're in respectable company here. Pardon my colleague, Monsieur. Three years ago he was a simple constable; he still hasn't learned good manners. Anyway, fine, it all seems a little fishy to me, but the girls are pretty and we give them the benefit of the doubt. Plus, the heat is murderous and I'm dying to stop for some liquid refreshment. We return their papers, the girls thank us before heading off for their train, all smiles after the nasty little scare we'd given them. So Cuvelier and me, we have a laugh and go for an anisette on a café terrace. And there, who do you think I see walk by, heading into the station we'd just left? A woman in her forties, looking upset, in a hurry, nervous – suspicious, in other words. And the thing is, she looks just like the two girls we'd just stopped. And she has that same Jew face. I get up and order Cuvelier to follow me. We catch up with her in the main hall. Police, your papers. Her card has the same surname as the two sisters, though her first name isn't Pauline, but most importantly, the pretty little word "Jewess" stamped in red letters. Cuvelier collars the lady while I run off to the platform. Another stroke of luck – the train for the Free Zone hasn't left yet. I give orders to stop it leaving and I inspect the carriages. I pick up the two girls and make them get off. March the whole little gang down to the station. And looking closer with the magnifying glass, you can see that the girls had "washed" their cards. So, if the mother hadn't had the lousy idea of giving her children a surprise send-off at the station, they'd have had us.'

'They'll have all the time in the world to think about that in Drancy,' Detective Cuvelier added. 'Family time.'

This story left me with a rather bitter aftertaste. But as I had told my daughter-in-law, that June night on Mont Saint-Michel, *France is occupied. Some people are responsible for this state of affairs, and now steps are being taken.* And you know as well as I do, Monsieur le Commandant – you can't make an omelette without breaking a few eggs.

Detective Cuvelier pointed to his colleague.

'You know, at headquarters they call Sadorski the "Jew-eater". But it seems that you're one, too. That's what they told us at the town hall, in any case. Is that so?'

I didn't answer. Inspector Sadorski leaned forward and said, 'Monsieur Husson, let me tell you the truth. In the national police, including General Inquiries, the pay is terrible. And to think some people are making a fortune these days! So to survive, we make ourselves a little on the side, you see. We protect people who might otherwise have certain problems with the law. Thanks to us, they have nothing to worry about. And as a token of their gratitude, they offer us a monthly stipend. For example, I know a certain Madame H. who works out of a little alleyway behind the arcades on Rue de Rivoli. Her profession is … how can I put it? Well, she makes pretty little angels, who go to Heaven before they get a chance to see what a rotten place this Earth can often be. Good for them, I say. And Madame H. helps an awful lot of people. Only, under the Maréchal, she's playing with fire. So I see to it that she's protected. As it happens, I dropped in last week to read the meter. The lady lives on the third floor. I was almost knocked down on the stairway by a young woman coming down at breakneck speed. I was just able to catch a glimpse of her face. As I told you, Monsieur Husson, I sometimes forget a name but *never a face*. And this one looked familiar ...'

Without asking permission, the Deputy Chief Inspector helped himself to more cognac.

'Unfortunately, a face without a name isn't much good to a police officer. But you know, my dear Monsieur, the world is a funny place. Take yesterday, on the café terrace outside the station – that Jew mother shows up right under our noses! Then, the cemetery caretaker's file lands on my desk the same week! And inside I find a press clipping from *Le Journal d'Andigny*. An article signed by Paul-Jean Husson. Well written, has some style to it. You gave him what for, that Lévy. But that name, the writer's, rang a bell. Husson, Paul-Jean ...'

He stopped to fix me with an ironic gaze. I was not at all happy with the turn the conversation – or rather, the monologue – had taken. I smiled.

'My family name is not uncommon.'

'Quite right. On the other hand, Paul-Jean is much less common than Jean-Paul. And strangely enough, somewhere in my bureaucratic mind, where everything is labelled and in its place, those names, first and last, *were linked with the face of the pretty blonde* I had run into on the angel-maker's stairway.'

I didn't understand, but I was growing more and more alarmed.

'My career in the French police suffered a setback a few years ago, Monsieur Husson. I was dismissed over some little fuss ... But now, I'm happy to say, they're hiring with a vengeance, and Commissioner Lang, who remembered my talents, reinstated me in his RG branch. In between, I'd been working for a private agency, located on Rue de la Lune in the second arrondissement of Paris. Next to the School of Wireless Telegraphy. Does that mean anything to you?'

I felt as if my heart had stopped beating.

And a new question almost immediately popped into my thoughts. A question that terrified me.

What had Ilse been doing in some squalid flat where secret abortions were taking place?

Sitting across from me as I broke out in a heavy sweat, Inspector Sadorski went on in his calm and vaguely insinuating tone.

'I speak Chancellor Hitler's language fluently, Monsieur Husson – my mother is from Alsace. It can be useful, especially nowadays. And that's why, back in '39, old man Dardanne thought of me for your little investigation in Berlin.'

'Ah, Berlin!' Detective Cuvelier echoed under his breath, either in envy or nostalgia. I hardly heard him. Cuvelier meant nothing to me – I was mistaken in that, as subsequent events were to demonstrate – and at that moment my eyes and ears were focused exclusively on his fearsome colleague Sadorski.

'I had the time to go through my old archives before we set off to see you, Monsieur Husson. The photo of the blonde wasn't very hard to find, nor was the corresponding file. The Wolffsohn/Berger case, *upon request of one Paul-Jean Husson*, 20 Quai de Verdun, Andigny, Département de l'Eure. All the pieces were falling into place. It was the same town the Commissioner was sending us to pick up the Jew! Quite amazing, but it made sense, and it gave me and my colleague here the chance to kill two birds with one stone, and save on petrol too ...'

I was too rattled to answer. Inspector Sadorski chuckled heartily and pulled a beige envelope from the pocket of his trench coat. And from that envelope he withdrew, with calculated slowness, a black-and-white photograph.

Elsie Berger, dressed in a ball gown, in *Das Flötenkonzert von Sans-souci*.

Detective Cuvelier leaned in for a closer look at the picture and whistled, not without reason. But I was in absolutely no mood to smile, let alone laugh. I desperately tried to think of some way to get us, my daughter-in-law and me, out of this indelicate situation. But first, I needed to understand the intentions of these men from the special branch of General Inquiries. They now knew that I was protecting an undeclared Jewess. I prayed that their only reason for visiting me in my home was to 'read the meter', as Sadorski had put it. Blackmail was the lesser of the potential perils in this story. So long as the demands of these swindlers remained within reasonable limits, I was quite capable of meeting them.

What was truly shattering to me was that my daughter-in-law had been caught visiting an abortionist.

'I had no trouble finding out that you are a widower with two children, Monsieur Husson – Jeanne, who died in an accident in 1938, and Olivier, not seen since his demobilisation in 1940. Where is your son at present? The Free Zone? London? North Africa?'

'I don't know. We've fallen out.'

'Not that we care, mind you. We work in the Jewish branch, not the political. What interests me about your son is that his wife, first name Ilse – well, well – still lives with her children at 10–12 Rue Richer, in Paris. She comes to see you here from time to time, they told us in town. So you haven't fallen out with her. During the week, she works as a secretary at the Opéra. Only the strange thing is, her naturalisation review file has gone missing. By chance? Or connections in high places?'

'I don't see what you're getting at. But yes, I do have friends in the Andigny Kreiskommandantur. And I know the Prefect of Police, Monsieur Langeron.'

'Who is no longer Prefect. And your friends at the Hôtel de Paris here are not the sort to take kindly to Jews. In fact, it was Commandant Schöllenhammer who called us to take custody of Lévy the caretaker. Okay, enough talking. This is what Cuvelier and I propose, Monsieur Husson. A little monthly payment of 5,000 francs. See how nice we are? In exchange, Madame Olivier Husson, née Wolffsohn, can sleep easy. And so can you.'

He held out his hand, palm upward.

'The first payment is effective immediately.'

I protested instinctively.

'I am not the kind of man who gives in to blackmail, Inspector.'

His colleague Cuvelier rose to his feet.

'Do you mind if I use your telephone? We need to send a car to pick up Madame Olivier Husson at her office at the Palais Garnier.'

'She'll be in Drancy by tomorrow,' Sadorski added. 'Along with the other foreigners of her religion. Undeclared, no star. That will be more than enough. And by the way, I happen to know that the representative of the French police in the Occupied Zone, Monsieur Leguay, is meeting SS Heinrichsohn today in Paris to discuss the forthcoming transports to the east. They're planning one a day by early September. A thousand Jews per train, sixty to a carriage, no seating.'

I gave in.

I asked my guests to wait while I went upstairs to fetch the money from my office.

I took the banknotes from my safe, slid them into an envelope and went back downstairs. Cuvelier was waiting for me midway up, looking furtive and sly. I walked by him without a word and handed the envelope to his superior, who stood sipping his cognac in the drawing room in front of the Boilly painting.

Inspector Sadorski pocketed the envelope and shook my hand. His grip was vigorous and firm. He smelled strongly of tobacco.

The two men returned to their Citroën and left with friendly waves in my direction. They were on their way to the Feldgendarmerie to pick up the Jew. We had agreed that Cuvelier would come to collect the next instalment in thirty days.

I closed the front door, went up to my room and lay on the bed to think.

22.

So Ilse had become pregnant with my offspring.

And without telling me, she had chosen to rid herself of the child she was carrying.

I had made myself the unwitting accomplice to *murder*. That of my own son, or daughter. A half-Jewish child, like Aristide and Hermione. Or even, in accordance with their own beliefs, fully Jewish.

Not only had I committed the carnal act with a woman of the accursed race that enjoined the torment of our Lord, and the wife of my own son, but this first and twofold sin had resulted in a far more serious act, a mortal sin, the most hateful of all sins. *Thanks to me, a woman had murdered her own child.*

I had brought about my own damnation.

And the just wrath of God was speeding me to Hell.

The guilt was entirely mine; yet again, I could not bring myself to blame Ilse.

Indeed, how would the poor woman have been able to explain to Olivier on his return – if he returned – the existence of another child? My daughter-in-law had acted, on her own behalf and from her own perspective, with wisdom. Every trace of our crime would have to be erased, *even if that meant committing another.*

The child – who would have been the half-brother or half-sister of my grandchildren, as well as their uncle or aunt – could not be allowed to come into the world.

Three oppressive days went by.

I was incapable of lifting a finger. Words and phrases would not come, making it impossible for me to write. My body was racked alternately by fever and icy shivering. The view of my dear hills, so supreme in their tranquillity, no longer succeeded in soothing my remorseful heart.

I couldn't eat; I couldn't sleep.

Filled with a nameless horror, I glanced often at the telephone. On the other end of the line were the flat on Rue Richer, the children I was no longer allowed to see, and Ilse, whom I loved, who had refused to speak to me for weeks, and to whom I dared not reveal what I knew – about my own crime and hers, about the abortionist on Rue de Rivoli, and the very fact of her Jewishness.

Outside, the weather was still as brutally hot and clear.

I burned in my own hell on Earth.

And I imagined that nothing worse could possibly befall me.

Yet it could.

On the third evening, towards 10.30 p.m., after the cook had gone home, I heard two imperious rings on the bell from the service door that opened onto Quai de Verdun.

I was still dressed.

I went down, but I was reluctant to open the door.

A voice I knew called out from the other side.

'Police! Detective Cuvelier! Come quickly, Monsieur Husson, it's an emergency!'

I immediately unlocked the door.

I was confused to see a car parked on the embankment, which was plunged in darkness because of the blackout. And two figures behind Cuvelier, who pushed me swiftly aside as he barged in.

The General Inquiries detective was pointing a small automatic pistol directly at me.

I backed away. Two men followed him in and closed the door behind them. In the light of the vestibule I saw a giant in a trench coat and a skinny fellow in a long black leather coat. He, too, had a handgun trained on me.

Later that night I got to know their nicknames: 'the Club' for the colossus and 'Simon' for the other. I was also to learn, by listening to them as they talked to one another, that the latter was a former policeman, jailed in Fresnes for some sort of civic corruption affair, and later released by someone they called, with fear-inflected respect, 'the Boss'. He pulled out a yellow card, stamped with the seal of the German eagle, and waved it at me briefly, barking, 'German police!' (although his accent could not have been more French).

'We're going to your office,' said Detective Cuvelier, who I noticed was carrying a leather briefcase in his left hand. 'You go first. Don't try anything stupid.'

Cuvelier, who had spoken in the polite, formal manner at our first meeting, was now using the familiar 'tu' with me. I didn't understand what was going on, but these men looked determined and fearsome. I had underestimated the threat posed by the 'Special Detective', who had seemed stupid beside his superior Sadorski. I wondered if these blackmailers were planning to kill me, pure and simple. As you know very well, Monsieur le Commandant, you hear all sorts of unpleasant stories these days, especially in the provinces. But they're usually about the settling of scores between police and terrorists or, as has always been the case since time immemorial, between one crook and another – and, by God's mercy, I am neither a crook nor a terrorist.

Climbing the stairs with the three men behind me, I argued with little conviction.

'If you represent the German police, Commandant Schöllenhammer and Dr Hild at the Kreiskommandantur can vouch for my respect for the law ...'

In response, I was hit in the lower back with a pistol grip and showered with vulgar insults.

The light was still on in my office. The colossus growled, 'Hurry up. Open the safe.'

Now I understood that I was dealing with common thieves acting behind the screen of their official functions. And, at the same time, that the 'Wolffsohn/Berger' affair was going to be more costly than I had foreseen.

Having little choice, I turned the dials on my safe.

The giant pushed me aside and helped himself to the contents: banknotes, securities, gold coins and, most painfully to me, Marguerite and Jeanne's jewellery, which I had been saving as keepsakes and not for their value, although that was significant. All found their way into the briefcase that Detective Cuvelier held out, wide open like the ravenous maw of a wild animal, to the oversized criminal whose massive hands, as broad as carpet-beaters, were shamelessly violating my most sacred treasures.

The man in the long leather coat – who, while far less solidly built than the giant, looked brutal and pitiless to me – turned to me and said, 'Now you're coming with us.'

I asked where.

'You'll see, Monsieur l'académicien,' Cuvelier snarled, shoving me in the ribs.

I threw on a jacket and an old cap. They made me get in the back of the car, a Citroën saloon like the last, although I don't know if it was the same one. Simon, the man in black, sat next to me, holding me at bay with his weapon. The detective took the wheel, with the Club filling up the entire space to his right.

We drove past the church. Two Feldgendarmes, their lapel pins glittering in the night, stepped out from behind the plane trees and waved their torches at the car, shouting '*Halt!*' and forcing us to a stop under threat of their submachine guns. The giant passed his own yellow card to the driver, who held it out through the lowered window. Your men saluted and stepped aside to let us by. From this I concluded that my kidnappers really did belong to some German police branch. In Paris, I had heard vague talk about a 'French Gestapo', also known as the Carlingue, an auxiliary service to yours headquartered on Rue Lauriston and run by Henri Lafont and Pierre Bonny – the latter a renowned former police inspector. I wondered if I had fallen into the hands of one of their teams, which were known for their summary methods.

The Citroën took a winding road that led up to the plateau. Up there, we passed through little sleeping villages, which I recognised despite the darkness: Cuverville, Houville-en-Vexin, Bacqueville ... The Club had a map that he had unfolded on his knees, and was giving directions to the detective, who at times appeared to be lost. I allowed myself an ironic quip.

'I know this area like the back of my hand, gentlemen. If you tell me where we are going, I can help you get there faster.'

'Are you really in such a hurry to wrap up our little excursion?'

The driver's response led me to believe that they were taking me into the deep countryside to kill me and bury my body in the undergrowth. Perhaps they would make me dig my own grave – I've heard about that sort of thing happening, too. I began to say my prayers in silence. I was not afraid for myself, believe me, Monsieur le Commandant. I came face to face with death many times, when climbing out of the trenches under a hail of bullets. I did not retreat or waver. But that night on the Vexin plateau, I was reluctant to leave this world and abandon Ilse, Hermione and Aristide, three innocents whom my son had already left exposed to the mercy of every peril.

We drove through Grainville, the last village before the town of Fleury-sur-Andelle. The saloon slowed down because, as I recalled very well, the road becomes increasingly steep at that point in its impressive plunge into the Andelle valley. A little further along, below and to the left, are the picturesque ruins of the Fontaine-Guérard abbey, which I visited last year with my family, and the Trappist monastery of Radepont. It's safer to stay under thirty kilometres an hour there, as the descent is punctuated by a series of extremely tight hairpin bends. And between each deadly turn are long and deceptive stretches of straight road through the forest, as if to tempt the unwary driver to step on the accelerator.

'Not too fast,' I counselled.

Simon, the former policeman sitting next to me, agreed.

'Laugnac warned us.'

'Anyway, we're here,' said the colossus in the front, folding his map up. 'I can see the dump, on the right.'

Cuvelier applied the brake and we slowed down. The moon was bright in the sky and a dark shadow rose up between the pines and beeches. I had driven past the house before and remembered it – isolated on the roadside halfway down the slope and overlooking the town through a break in the tree line. A strange-looking heap, somewhere between a castle and a post house – too small for the one, too big for the other – mysterious and gloomy, somewhat dilapidated with its dark brick walls, its crumbling turret roofs, its broken lightning rods, its eternally closed and rotting shutters. It felt ill-omened, as if ancient crimes and other macabre incidents had occurred there. I had considered featuring it in any number of scenes in my novels, but had always ended up rejecting the idea, seized with some superstitious fear that the evil aura surrounding the place might somehow insinuate itself into my writing, and perhaps even into me or those I loved.

A Renault Vivasport with a rear gas generator and another black Citroën saloon were parked outside the house, their headlights extinguished. And, most unexpectedly, a bright light shone through the shutter slats of a window on the second floor. Cuvelier pulled up behind the Vivasport and turned off the headlights.

'Everyone out,' he said jauntily.

The Club pushed open the front door, which was not locked. All four of us went inside, where I was immediately struck by the smell of cigarette smoke, mingled with a whiff of mould and the excrement of forest creatures. As I had always thought, the house was uninhabited – empty rooms, bare walls, loose wallpaper, light fixtures covered in dust. Spider webs in every corner, mouse and ferret droppings strewn across warped floorboards. But I heard voices upstairs. We climbed an old stairway, its boards squeaking. Above us, the light was on in one room. That's where the voices were coming from. On the landing, the man in the black coat beside me let out a yell in a false German accent: '*Kamerad!*'

The door to the room, already ajar, opened wider.

The first thing I saw was a man sitting on a chair, entirely naked.

His wrists and his ankles were cuffed.

23

There was something theatrical about the scene which lay before me, beneath the glittering light of a chandelier.

The high walls of the enormous room were hung with nineteenth-century family portraits that had been slashed with a knife. The room was furnished only with an armchair and a few upright chairs; a metal bucket and suitcase sat on the floor. And in the middle, a handsome young man of good height in the tailored black uniform and boots of an SS officer, wearing a cap that was too big for him and armed with a riding crop, stood contemplating the prisoner.

A third person – the one who had opened the door for us – of very small stature, almost a dwarf, dark-brown complexion, stubbled chin, his repulsive ugliness accentuated by one blank, blind eye, chuckled as he swung what looked to be a sock filled with sand that served as a truncheon.

The face of their victim was swollen, his torso marbled with long purple streaks. Naked and bound, the boy could not have been more than twenty years old. His features, despite the signs of the violence that had distorted them, reminded me of someone I had known a long time ago ... But who? I was too disturbed to be able to focus on the question.

The SS officer fixed us with a hard but intelligent gaze and spoke French with Norman intonations, and I realised that the only German thing about him was his uniform. His name, Monsieur le Commandant, is Martin Laugnac. Later that night, Detective Cuvelier explained to me that he is deputy to Hauptscharführer Harald Heyns (also known as 'Bernard') in the Gestapo security office in Caen. Laugnac was a junior tax clerk before the war. His admiration for the Maréchal, and his attraction to the German uniform, drew him to the company of the officers of the Feldkommandantur. As a speaker of your language, he was soon recruited as a police interpreter.

The young man seemed to be on close terms with Simon and the Club, as he and the dwarf welcomed them with much laughter and joking. Having saluted the detective, the French SS officer shook me by the hand, with a certain degree of respect, and called me 'Commandant Husson', adding that he had read my novel *The Ordeal*. His brown eyes, deeply sunk in their sockets, shone with a strange fervour.

Pointing to the only armchair, the officer politely invited me to sit down.

He turned back to the boy in handcuffs and ordered him to introduce himself.

The prisoner, who seemed to be all but drained of strength, raised his head. I again had the feeling that I recognised his face.

'Your surname and Christian name,' Laugnac repeated impatiently. 'My Parisian guests are waiting.'

He emphasised the command by lashing him across the chest with the crop. In a weak voice, the young man muttered, 'Pin, André.'

'Born in?' the officer went on.

The boy shuddered.

'Fresne-l'Archevêque.'

I knew the village – as do you, of course, since it is only about ten kilometres from Andigny. But the name 'Pin' also rang a bell. I combed through my memories, one of which, leaping suddenly to mind, alarmed me.

'What is your father's profession, my poor boy?' I asked him gently, leaning forward in the armchair.

'Constable,' he answered.

Drops of sweat broke out on my forehead as I silently calculated, dredging up old dates.

'Your maternal grandfather,' I went on. 'What is his trade?'

'He had a café in the village. He died just before the defeat.'

'And ... your mother's Christian name?'

With a sob, he said, 'Madeleine.'

It wasn't possible. And yet, I was already saying 'tu' to him.

'What year were you born?'

'Nineteen twenty-two.'

A heavy stone with sharp edges tore at something within my chest. Now I understood why his face had looked so familiar.

He looked just like me when I was twenty.

Madeleine's features slowly swam into focus as I stared at the wretched young man in the chair. A brief affair, unknown to Marguerite, in the years after the Great War, with a café owner's daughter. She fell pregnant and I had arranged for her to marry the local constable, a strapping man as yet unmarried. I never saw Madeleine again after the wedding ... The others in the room had no idea; judging by their obtuse or curious expressions, I deduced that the theatrical scene had not been staged with the ironic and perverse aim of bringing father and son face to face as prisoners of this dreadful place. It was just another, cruelly treacherous stroke of the fate that had been cleverly toying with me for years.

From the next room came the sound of a slap, followed by a jostling of bodies. I thought I heard a woman's voice cry out. We all turned our heads in that direction. The door opened, and two new people entered the room.

A tall young woman with long, curly chestnut hair was shoved in by a scrawny kid with a light moustache. Her hands were cuffed behind her back. She wore only a white underskirt and a brassiere of the same colour, and on her feet a pair of burgundy high heels. I noticed that, oddly, her hands were gloved – rather elegant short gloves of cream-coloured leather.

The girl had a black eye, and blood ran down her thighs.

I knew the young man with the moustache. He was an activist in the Andigny PPF whom I had seen running the propaganda and recruitment programme for the Legion of French Volunteers. In a triumphant voice he declared: 'The girl woke up. It was great, lads! She still had her cherry, at twenty-three …'

Then he saw me and shut up, embarrassed.

The wall-eyed dwarf uncuffed the young woman, made her sit in a chair, tied her arms behind her back with a rope, and then strapped her by the chest, keeping it arched against the back of the chair. The dwarf's movements were remarkably quick and precise, as were his knotting skills. His prisoner let out a moan. She stared at each of us in turn with a wild look on her face, still in shock from the defilement the poor child had just been subjected to. Tears had left tracks down her swollen face. It was a rather pretty face. Detective Cuvelier sniggered beside me.

Martin Laugnac then turned to my son – for that is what I shall call him from now on, young André Pin whom I had never seen until this moment, as an adult. The SS officer punched him squarely in the face, knocking his head backwards.

Laugnac asked my son, whose nose had begun to bleed, where the Allied airmen who had been shot down near Mesnil-Raoul were now hiding. He replied in a whisper that he didn't know anything about it.

The officer slapped him twice across the face, and said, 'Too bad for her.'

'But good for us,' Cuvelier cackled, eliciting laughter from the others.

Laugnac walked over to the suitcase and opened the lid. Inside, I saw more rope and various implements, scissors, hammers and spikes. He withdrew a large scourge, which had been customised with a series of knots to augment its efficacy – as he was pleased to point out. He then began to lash the legs, thighs, forearms and shoulders of his female captive. The blood quickly began to flow, and wherever the blows fell twice in the same place they flayed the skin, exposing raw flesh. The young woman screamed until I thought my heart would break. I wanted to get up, put an end to the horrific scene, but Simon continued, with a smile, to point his automatic at me. The officer rested; his arm was tired.

'Surname, Christian name,' he ordered, panting.

Her head on her chest, his victim sobbed. Grabbing her by the hair, he pulled her face upwards.

'I won't say it twice …'

'Lelouarn, Yvonne.'

'Address.'

'Avenue du Maréchal Foch, number eleven … In Evreux.'

'What does your father do?'

'He's a pharmacist …'

'What's your network?'

'I'm not in the Resistance! I swear!'

The SS officer raised his voice above hers.

'What about the false identity cards we found on you?' (He then called her by names that I shall not transcribe.)

'Someone gave them to me … I was helping out …'

'Do you think we were born yesterday? So who gave them to you?'

She lowered her eyes without answering. Laugnac punched her. Blood spurted from her mouth.

The officer bellowed: 'We know you're in the Rainbow Network! Filthy terrorist c**t! Give us the names!'

He continued to hurl insults at her. The scourge fell again, tearing off strips of flesh. The blood streamed across her white skirt, down her legs ... Sitting in the armchair, I trembled. I saw many dreadful things in the Great War, Monsieur le Commandant, but I had never seen a woman being tortured. My heart beat furiously, I felt sick to my stomach, my knees knocked together, my hands trembled. I beseeched the good Lord to put an end to her suffering.

Beside himself, Laugnac threw the scourge across the room. He bent over, tore the shoes off Yvonne Lelouarn and began to stamp on her bare feet with his heavy boots. I closed my eyes, and I heard him break her ankles. Immediately afterwards, he shouted, 'She's all yours, José.'

The dwarf approached the young woman, delicately took her one hand, and then the other, and pulled off the gloves. I watched him select a long lancet from among the implements in the valise, take the index finger of her right hand and plunge the instrument under its nail. The poor wretch howled like a wounded animal. We all watched in silence – horrified in the case of André and myself, fascinated in that of the others. When the wailing tapered off, the dwarf took up a second finger and inserted a second lancet. Leaving it in, he grabbed hold of the nail and ripped it off.

'Stop,' Laugnac interrupted. 'Let's first ask Pin if he wants José to do all the fingers ... and then the other hand.'

My son was weeping quietly. The young man in uniform bent over him. It occurred to me that they were more or less the same age.

'Where are the airmen? If you tell me where they're hidden I'll stop the whole thing. We'll take Mademoiselle Lelouarn for treatment in the infirmary at Caen prison. I will ensure that she is seen to. In a month or two, she'll be free to rejoin her family in Evreux. We are not monsters. Personally, it saddens me to see a young compatriot who was naïve enough to fall for propaganda being treated this way because of those bastards who chuck bombs at French homes ... Do you have any idea how many civilians have been killed? Bodies torn to shreds? Women, children ...'

André did not respond.

'Call yourself a man?' Laugnac muttered. 'How can you bear to see that girl suffer because of you? When all you have to do is say two words to save her. The name of the farm. The name of the village.'

My son shook his head. The officer stood up straight and sighed.

'José!'

The dwarf returned, with his lancets.

Four bloody fingernails had been flung to the floor before my son cried out for them to stop.

He gave the names of a farmer and a village.

Laugnac ordered the youngster from the PPF to take notes.

'And then you'll take down the other names,' he added.

I didn't understand. Cuvelier chuckled behind me.

'Once they start to sing ...'

The Club stepped forward. The dwarf removed the handcuffs from André's wrists. The giant picked up my son, dragged him to the door that led to the next room, and raised him up. Cuvelier and Simon grabbed one arm each and raised them towards the lintel of the door. The dwarf ran up with a chair.

Laugnac had taken a mallet and two long black nails from the valise. He stepped onto the chair. I made as if to stand up, but the PPF fellow drew a pistol and forced me to stay seated in the armchair.

How can I write this?

Monsieur le Commandant. They nailed my son's hands to the lintel. The blood-drenched girl, tied to the chair, wailed and wept.

I stood. The little fellow with the moustache hit me with the butt of his gun and I fell forward. I passed out.

*

When I opened my eyes, I was back in the armchair. I heard a series of steady blows.

Detective Cuvelier grunted as he lashed my son, still hanging, across the back with a belt. The buckle had turned his back into one great open wound of bleeding flesh, in which the shredded muscles were clearly visible. André seemed to be unconscious.

The dwarf amused himself by circling the young woman and pricking the skin of her neck and throat with the tip of a long kitchen knife. Simon ordered him to step aside and emptied the bucket of water over Mademoiselle Lelouarn. Detective Cuvelier stopped lashing the suspended André for a moment and turned to watch. Laugnac approached his prisoner, who dripped with water and blood. He gave her two sharp slaps.

'Now, give us the names of your accomplices in the network. If you don't, we'll kill him, take him down and nail you up there in his place. Talk now before it's too late ... Before we get *really* mean.'

Simon, the former policeman, approached in turn.

'I'd talk if I were you, sweetie. These Gestapo boys from Caen are tough. I've seen them cut strips of skin off the soles of their suspect's feet. And the really stubborn ones who still resist – well, it's too bad for them. Laugnac and José reward them by sewing their mouths shut with wire. Is that what you want them to do to you? Think of your poor mother ...'

He waited, gazing at her mildly. He stroked her cheek. A few seconds later the girl mumbled a name. An address. Then another name. And another address ...

The PPF fellow feverishly wrote in his notebook. Sometimes she went too fast for him. Laugnac rubbed his hands together.

When she had finished, they took André Pin down. They laid him out on his stomach to spare his ruined back. I prayed under my breath. I said the Our Father. Then I got up and went to kneel by my son, stroking his head. I looked at his hands, punctured like those of Our

Lord. My tears fell, and I could do nothing to stop them. I cried for my son. For Yvonne Lelouarn. For Ilse and her children. For the French, and for myself, too.

The men dragged the young woman into the next room. They raped her one after the other – all except Martin Laugnac, who stayed in the large room, sitting across from me and studying me in silence – before bringing her back, naked and dishevelled, covered in blood and semen. They had to hold her by the underarms because of her broken ankles. Her eyes were completely unfocused. Stupefied, she was already gone, far away.

Laugnac picked up my son.

'Follow us. We're going for a stroll in the woods.'

André could barely walk.

'Let me write a letter to my parents first,' he begged. 'Please … And I also want to say goodbye to my little sister Germaine …'

I heard the giant cackle.

'With those hands? You couldn't even draw a cross.'

André's fingers were all twisted and crooked. I offered to write the letter for him, at his dictation. I promised to bring it to Fresnel'Archevêque myself, if I were allowed.

'No time,' Laugnac decreed. 'We have to take care of these two, call for reinforcements, and head over to the farm to nab those Brits. I'll go and see your mother. I'll tell her myself that you ratted on everyone and then died like a dog.'

'Bastard,' I shouted.

He smiled.

'It was a pleasure to make your acquaintance, Commandant Husson.'

Detective Cuvelier grabbed me by the shoulders and pulled me back.

The others left the room. I heard a door slam downstairs, then the car doors, and the two vehicles sped away.

24.

Simon and the Club returned to find me slumped in the armchair, under the watchful eye of the detective.

The three men lit cigarettes, sat on the chairs, which were still spattered with blood, and laid out their demands.

The plan had changed since the last time. It was no longer a matter of 5,000 a month. I now had ten days to gather and deliver a single payment of 250,000 francs. That is no small sum, Monsieur le Commandant, and I did not have it. But these crooks had done their homework. As I have mentioned, my marriage to Marguerite had brought me two buildings in Paris. By mortgaging one I could quickly borrow what I needed, and later, if necessary, repay the bank by selling the other. My thieving blackmailers knew it, and so did I.

If I refused to pay, they would fetch Ilse from Rue Richer, bring her to the house of sorrows in Fleury-sur-Andelle, and leave her with Martin Laugnac and his men. Who would be very happy to have a Jewess to play with, according to the Club. Nailing people to beams is one of their favourite pastimes. These police auxiliaries trawl the province picking up Resistance or black-market suspects in their cars. They sometimes pass themselves off as dissidents, entrapping farmers or tradesmen with Resistance sympathies. Those who they do not kill on the spot in a hail of bullets they bring to the sort of place I had been taken to. Their bodies, buried in remote forests or flung down the deepest wells, are never found.

I accepted their conditions. What choice did I have?

These men had me.

I did not know whether Cuvelier had arranged all this without Sadorski's knowledge. It was very likely – in which case, he intended to slip him his share of the 5,000 every month and claim he had received it from me.

What difference did it make? No matter how you looked at it, I was trapped.

Here I must digress a moment.

No one believed more than I did, and still do, Monsieur le Commandant, in the importance and the future of Collaboration between our two peoples. How could I write you such a letter, in confidential friendship, if I did not?

I deeply respect the warrior's uniform you wear. You and I are of the same rank, for that matter. Like my compatriots, it pains me to see that uniform, the uniform of the German Army, sullied by acts that you yourself would never commit, but which others who are not German undertake by exploiting and abusing the considerable authority that you undoubtedly erred in conferring upon them. Such men, who just nights ago I heard identify themselves to your Feldgendarmes as agents of the German secret police, deserve no other title but *thieves, extortionists, murderers* ...

If these flocks of gallows birds are allowed to run wild in our country with impunity, the Collaboration, that great endeavour, may well be compromised in my province and elsewhere. The integration of France into Europe must be more than an empty promise, a rhetorical flourish. It must be a tangible reality, accessible to all. Alongside its political and technical transformation, French society must be transformed *morally*. Your Ambassador, His Excellency Monsieur Otto Abetz – and I intend to write him a memorandum on this subject – would be well advised to demand the dismissal or apprehension of these wayward auxiliaries, as well as a 'cleansing' of corrupt elements who dishonour the French

Police. Franco-German relations would thereby be completely overhauled, and men who, like me, are resolved to see the triumph of the policy of Collaboration in France would be ideally empowered to confound their enemies and rally their partisans.

Has your Chancellor himself not written: 'We Aryans can conceive of the State only as a living organism that not only ensures the continuity of the race but cultivates its intellectual and creative capacities to their highest degree of freedom and fulfilment'?

The Führer would surely not gainsay me if I were to add that freedom and development can flourish only in a dynamic that is both *spiritual* and *moral*.

A few days later, I plucked up my courage and placed a call to Rue Richer.

As usual, Hermione answered the phone. I asked her firmly to let me speak to her mother. My granddaughter hesitated. I therefore asked her to inform her mother that it was about *a certain lady she had visited on the third floor of a building off Rue de Rivoli ...*

A moment later, I heard Ilse's voice – for the first time in so long! – at the end of the line. It was muted and trembling. I heard her send Hermione from the room, and then she began by begging me to forgive her.

'It was so awful. I didn't want to do it, but ...'

In my most affectionate and reassuring voice, I gently reproached her for not having told me about her pregnancy. And then I asked her how she had found that woman.

'It was Odette who ... One of the dancers at the Opéra. They sometimes have that sort of problem. She asked one of her friends. And when I got the information, I made an appointment and went over there ...'

Deeply moved, I assured my daughter-in-law that had I not had certain religious principles I should have liked to be there with her.

I heard her sobbing on the other end.

'Can you ever forgive me, Paul-Jean? I climbed the stairs, I rang … That horrible old woman came to the door. The flat smelled bad. Behind the old lady was a table covered in a filthy chequered cloth. Water was boiling in a pot. I saw long knitting needles …'

Mortified and sickened, I held my breath.

'And then … I couldn't do it, I turned around. I ran down the stairs, knocked into some man, into the street … I took the bus …'

My fist gripped the receiver. And there was I imagining that the whole affair was long past! Stammering, I interrupted her story.

'What do you mean …? You didn't go through with it? Are you still …?'

She was astonished. 'But I thought it was that woman who told you … Otherwise, how would you have known?'

'It doesn't matter. But then … What are you going to do?'

Silence. My daughter-in-law began to cry. Between sobs, I heard her say: 'I don't know … It is already eleven weeks.'

I buried my face in my hands. It was unbelievable, horrendous – *every time I thought myself free from this nightmare it started up all over again*! I tried to think, but no solution came to mind for the moment. I decided to play for time. I asked her if she didn't want to keep the child. Ilse began shouting.

'Don't even think of it! What about your son? … You must understand, I love Olivier. I love him, *I love him*, he's my one and only and I'm waiting for him to come home to me!'

And she added, 'Yes, it's my fault. I'm an idiot. But I don't want to lose your son because of one silly mistake.'

That hurt me. A *silly mistake*. The apogee of my extraordinary love, the miracle consecrated by the Holy Mount, *on* the Holy Mount, that unique and unimpeachable communion of our flesh and our souls

– that's what Ilse called a *silly mistake*!

I muttered a few befuddled words, promised to call back the next day, and hung up.

I thought about it for a few minutes, then picked up the phone and asked the operator to connect me to the German Institute in Paris. Luckily, Lieutenant Heller was still in the office he has occupied since his section was transferred from the Champs-Élysées. I needed to attack my problems one at a time. I thought that perhaps this young, well-educated officer, whom I knew to have good connections, might help me avoid having to pay off my blackmailers. I asked if he might see me the next day – that is, yesterday, Monsieur le Commandant. When we were alone together, and without mentioning anything about my daughter-in-law, I explained that I was being blackmailed by French police officers and former officers carrying the yellow cards, possibly counterfeit, of Gestapo auxiliaries. I gave him their full names, and described the colossus Club. Lieutenant Heller promised to do whatever he could. He immediately placed several phone calls, speaking in German. His face darkened as he spoke. His last interlocutor shouted so loudly that I could clearly hear his expletives from where I sat. The lieutenant hung up, sighed, and opened his arms in a gesture of impotence.

'I spoke to the diplomatic envoy, Rahn. It's just as I feared. Your conmen are working for a man named Henri Chamberlin, alias Lafont. A crook, but one who belongs to our secret police. His services are critical to our counter-terrorism efforts. On our authority, this Lafont had a band of criminals released from Fresnes prison to serve as his assistants, because such men are efficient, without scruple and experienced. Yet dishonest by nature, as you have learned to your cost. You must understand that these Frenchmen are very useful to us in repressing terrorism. Our occupying forces are too few and could never manage it on their own. We are waging a difficult war in the East that is taking up much of our manpower. So it's important that we have Frenchmen working for us. If you only knew how many denunciation letters I get! Some of them signed by your most reputable colleagues or their wives. You'd be surprised.' He lowered his voice. 'Others, unfortunately, are engaged in regrettable activities, such as Monsieur Paulhan, or the excellent poet Monsieur Desnos. For their own safety, I do hope those gentlemen don't push their luck.' He sighed sorrowfully. 'As to your case, to put it bluntly, I have just been informed to mind my own business. Which is literature, not police work. Believe me, I am truly sorry, Monsieur Husson.'

25.

Just nights ago I lost another son – André Pin, who looked so much like I did at twenty and who died practically before my eyes, with the heroic courage of a martyr.

If he talked under torture, it was only in the hope – sadly illusory – that the monsters who were tormenting the young dissident woman would spare her at least, if only by setting aside their diabolical implements.

I would have done the same thing if I had been in his place, Monsieur le Commandant. Yes, I would have given names without hesitating! Whilst it handed a death sentence to a farmer and some airmen who were on the same side as André, and probably to himself as well – for my son surely knew that the torturers rid themselves of anyone who was no longer useful to them – his decision was in the purest chivalric tradition of our land, because it sprang from universal compassion, the defence of a maiden, the duty to protect the weakest among us.

I was proud of André.

Proud of the unknown son whom I discovered for the first time only to lose him the same night.

I felt a savage destiny closing in on me; I was losing my children one by one.

Jeanne drowned, Olivier disowned, André murdered …

Three entirely French children. Born in France to decent Christian families.

My French family was crumbling around me. And I was left alone. Alone?

No, quite the opposite, because new elements were appearing and growing.

I would even say, *proliferating*.

Impure elements, 100 per cent Jewish or half-Jewish. Ilse. Hermione. Aristide. And now a new seed was developing in my daughter-in-law's belly that was half-Semitic and, worst of all, conceived in the double sin of incest and adultery!

Was not the invisible being growing inexorably in Ilse's flesh both the monstrous, demonic embodiment of my crime, and the instrument of my punishment?

I did not want that child to see the light of day. My reasons were very different from those of my daughter-in-law, but the result would be the same. On the other hand, my religion, my beliefs – my sense of morality – forbade me from destroying it. And in any case, no crime can be redeemed by another crime!

I had been appropriately damned and punished for all that I had done to date. Through the cruel, successive blows He had dealt me, Our Lord had shown me, like the writing on the wall, the extent and abomination of my sins.

I considered the situation in despair.

If the path to a new crime was forbidden me, that meant that *God had decreed that the child should live.*

But it could not live as a member of my family. Neither Olivier nor Ilse would endure it. And I understood my German daughter-in-law well enough to know that she would never consent to entrust the child to strangers, either. As upright and sincere as she was, the idea of concealing from her husband – *the man she loved*, as she had so cruelly reminded me – the existence of a secret child would have been totally inconceivable to her.

Ultimately, as in mathematics, this dreadful equation had but one solution.

And I found it.

The one, final solution that would also free me – although it was only a secondary concern – from the grip of my blackmailers, pulling the rug from beneath their feet by removing the sole source of power they held over me.

Do you understand, Monsieur le Commandant?

In writing you this letter, I am placing the fate of Ilse Husson in your hands.

Yes, it is to you, in all faith and friendship, dear Commandant Schöllenhammer, that I entrust the fates of the woman I love and the child, my own, that she carries in her womb.

Your Reich is opening new spaces in Eastern Europe that it is reserving for the Jewish race in order to offer a final, and humane, solution to the eternal problem of the Jew.

As a member of the elite corps of the SS, you are the vanguard of your Nation.

A high-ranking officer, you have power, good judgement and influence. You will certainly be able to place my daughter-in-law in the construction zone best suited to her situation as a young mother.

I have no doubt, of course, that it will be hard on her. I am not so naïve as to believe that the workers' camps in the new territories of the East are restful resorts. But the Jewish people have sinned too, and they must henceforth learn, as we French are learning, to bend their backs and wield shovel and pick.

The Jews were able to corrupt or unman a nation because it is easy to break things down. And yet we had laws. But the people slipped through their net, or rather dripped. It is easy to leak away when one has been liquefied.

No need for new laws! We need only to enforce the ones we have. Or to increase the penalties threefold if you want to speed things up. Make examples. One threat and you'll see them obey. When you have these two powers over men – the ability to terrify them and the ability to buy them – you have them where you want them. Fear is the parent of virtue. And when fear has them firmly in its grip, we will be there to provide them with the sublime motives for leading a moral life. Repression fails when it dies on the road. The Spanish did away with heresy in the sixteenth century. But you have to really want it. To have the moral strength. Behind your material strength, Monsieur le Commandant, you had moral strength aplenty, and it was that more than anything that defeated us! Give us a little of your strength, give the French the passion to forbid, to punish, not to yield! The men of France must today, here and now, nurture within themselves all the virtues related to strength, quality and self-control, with particular stress on those virtues that they have most been lacking – the manly virtues.

Let us not deceive ourselves. Merely injecting a little order into things is not the same as bringing about a National Revolution. Dusting off the old virtues is not bringing about a revolution. To bring about a revolution is to forge a new morality. And to do so without compunction. However useful they may be at any given moment, ideas and morality, when applied at the wrong time, no longer merit compunction.

In a new system, France must assume the place that, long before the trial by strength, she had earned for herself – defeat was but one sign amongst other, less dramatic signs. She must understand that the right of the victor over the vanquished is limited only by the victor's interests (not a single voice, even among the least tainted, has been raised against the prerogatives of conquest or, for that matter, against the war itself). She must understand that Franco-German relations will be fruitful only if they are played out in the same revolutionary climate that gave birth to Hitler's Germany, since what we have gone through and endured, and what we will go through and endure, will have meaning only in the context of the genuine revolution that is at stake in this war.

For once, we shall have to be good losers. No weeping and wailing, no sulking, no childish base revolt passed off as patriotism, when in fact it is an insult to the word. It was *before* and *during* that we should have harassed the enemy, not *after*. We must not meet the future with bad grace. We have to take the broad view and say yes, wholeheartedly, to the events of 1940. A double acceptance of reality as it is and of a just outcome – we were beaten fair and square, and at every level. Having accepted the facts, we must embrace them. We wallowed in abundance for twenty years; I see no reason to complain about going without for a few more. The people of Paris watched as German troops marched up the Champs-Élysées. These are the vagaries of History. These are the tides of the universe.

Many times we heard it said that night would fall upon the entire world should you prevail by force of arms. But night after night since the world began, night has fallen upon the world.

Quite the opposite, it was Our Lord Jesus Christ who returned, riding the victor's chariot. He entered by one gate, while his co-religionists – I am not so simple or hypocritical to forget that he was a Jew – were swept out by another.

One does not reach the light in a single journey.

One reaches it via a darkling road.

I am well aware, Monsieur le Commandant, that Ilse will suffer. And I, too, terribly, from this definitive separation.

If Olivier makes it back, I will explain it to him.

You know as well as I do that the Jewish element is one that is foreign to our people, to our race, to our homeland. Events, general and specific, have amply demonstrated that to be true. What we must all do now is return to our proper places.

On his return, my son shall choose a French, Christian wife. Many young men have died, alas, and many more will die before the end of hostilities. Unattached women are not lacking in our country.

Beautiful and intelligent, Ilse shall in turn readily find a new male of her race who will impregnate her again. And the child yet to be born, which I allow her to take with her, will gradually acquire the place in her heart of those, my grandchildren, left behind in France.

The members of this new family will labour, pioneers of a virgin soil, to build themselves a healthy life, rich in promise.

Last night, I called my daughter-in-law, as planned.

I told her that I had found a doctor willing to deal with her delicate situation discreetly. This Dr Larrieu is younger than Dr Dimey and has no qualms about lending himself to my little stratagem. I am certain of his unwavering loyalty to the Maréchal, and you and I can count on his discretion.

Ilse and her children will arrive at Andigny station tomorrow, in the early afternoon. I'll be waiting there with my car. We will first drop Hermione and Aristide at the villa, where the servants will watch them until my return. The appointment with Dr Larrieu is at 3.30 p.m. I will leave Ilse there, promising to be back for her in two hours. I will kiss her goodbye.

Only I will know that it is our final farewell.

The receptionist will keep my daughter-in-law in the waiting room until your police officers come for her. In the meanwhile, I shall have gone to the Sainte-Blandine Institute, where I have enrolled Hermione as a boarding student for the coming year, and whose headmistress, a saintly woman, fully understands the situation as I have explained it to her. Two Sisters will accompany me to Villa Némésis to retrieve my granddaughter and to calm the poor child's inevitable fears. But I know I can count on time, which soothes all pain, and on the infinite patience of our good and benevolent Sisters. I have arranged everything as far as Aristide is concerned, too, having found him a wet nurse, my cook's niece, in the next village.

Naturally, I shall have Hermione home with me on school holidays, and my grandson, too, in a few years.

All that remains, Monsieur le Commandant, is for me to seal this letter in an envelope addressed to you. Later, I shall make one last call to my daughter-in-law to confirm our appointment tomorrow.

Please forgive me, my dear friend, for having taken the liberty today of begging the honour of your assistance. It all comes down to one cause: my great misfortune and desire to save, despite herself, a remarkable woman who is the innocent victim of a complex and frightful situation.

I commend Ilse to you, Monsieur le Commandant. Treat her well and never forget that, despite everything, *I still love her*.

I beg of you, please tell the men who will arrest her to do their duty as gently as possible.

Look on her as a simple traveller, returning to her homeland there in the East to accept her just reward of a more peaceful and better world.

Please forgive me, Monsieur le Commandant, for having burdened you with these lengthy yet, you will agree, necessary explanations, and be assured of my most devoted and respectful regard for you.

Most sincerely,

Paul-Jean Husson

DOCUMENT 1[14]

TELEGRAM

Paris, 1 October 1940, 9.45 p.m.
Received: 1 October 1940, 10 p.m., No. 740.

Solving the Jewish problem in the Occupied Zone of France will require, among a variety of other measures, the speediest possible settlement of the issue of the nationality of German Jews living here before the war, whether they were interned or not. Up to now, the process for individual forfeiture of nationality has been based on paragraph 2 of the law of 14 July 1933 and exclusively targeted violations of sworn allegiance, without taking racial identity into account. For the future, I would suggest a process for collective forfeiture of nationality in the Occupied Zone of France on the basis of the lists drawh up here by mutual agreement with the Hoheitsträger.[15] Such lists should include first and foremost the members of the following groups:

1. So called ex-Austrian Jews, namely, those persons who, following circular R.17.178 of 20 August 1938, failed to exchange their Austrian passports for German before 31 December 1938.

2. German Jews of the Reich who, by failing to take part in the census, are in violation of paragraph 5 of the law of 3 February 1938 on the compulsory registration of members of the German State abroad.

The proposed measures should be considered only as a first step towards resolving the Jewish problem as a whole. I reserve the right to offer further proposals. Request approval by telegraph.

Signed: ABETZ

19 copies sent

DOCUMENT 2

AMBASSADOR ABETZ
Paris, 1 March 1941

Note for Herr Zeitschel

To the list of French collaborators with the Central Jewish Office, please add the names of Marcel Bucard, Darquier de Pellepoix, Jean Boissel and Pierre Clémenti, of whom we spoke earlier today, as well as the writers Serpeille de Gobineau, Jean de la Hire, Paul-Jean Husson,[16] Ferdinand[17] Céline and the Comte de Puységur.

As persons likely to do truly effective work, I recommend university professor Montandon and the writer Jacques de Lesdain.

The deputy head of the Propagandastaffel, Sonderführer von Grothe, will launch inquiries in other sectors to identify French citizens who may be amenable to cooperating with the Central Jewish Office.

Signed: ABETZ

DOCUMENT 3

Transcript from the documentary film *Elsie Bergers Französische Familie* (*Elsie Berger's French Family*), produced by Peter Klemm for German television.

Interview with Monsieur François Lefèvre, retired, former member of the French Resistance movement Francs-Tireurs Partisans.

PETER KLEMM: *What was the economic status of Andigny at the outbreak of the war?*
FRANÇOIS LEFÈVRE: It was a pretty middle-class town. You couldn't really call it an industrial town, since it only had the glassworks and the silk trade. It was a market town, a big market town, but not a city. It had a population of 5,600 in 1936, and people thought more like country folk than city folk.
P.K.: *Were there any foreigners?*
F.L.: Yes, especially Spaniards in the 1930s. But it wasn't a large community. Their presence didn't bother anybody. That is to say, there was never any hostility towards them, other than a few articles in *Le Journal d'Andigny*.
P.K.: *And Jews?*
F.L.: I only knew Monsieur Lévy, who worked as caretaker at the cemetery. He was a veteran of the First World War. He was deported. The other Jews were Parisians who had country houses on the Seine. They wore the yellow star, but we only saw them here on holiday. They thought they were free to travel as they liked if they

wore the star. But some of them were arrested in Paris, like that engineer who died in Auschwitz, along with his wife, and one of their daughters died of typhus in Bergen-Belsen.

P.K.: *And politically?*

F.L.: There were communists like me, and some Croix-de-Feu[18] members. And a few excitable youngsters in the PPF. There was even one who signed up to fight on the Eastern Front, with the Germans; you saw him swaggering around town on leave in his German uniform. Well, off he went and he never came back; he might've been one of those who was picked up at the end of the war and shot by the French army … But there were no physical confrontations between the communists and the far right in Andigny. They had their own ideas, but they respected each other as Frenchmen. The only 'clashes' were between *Le Patriote* and *Le Journal d'Andigny*. It was just a war of words between newspapers. The Germans shut down the *Patriote* in '42, since it had always leaned towards the Popular Front. But in any case the *Journal*, with its conservative Old France sympathies, had a wider readership because it was more in tune with local feeling. Its owner was a rabid collaborator, and she had some trouble with the law after the liberation.

P.K.: *Did the air raid on 8 June 1940 trigger a mass exodus?*

F.L.: A lot of people left, maybe 30 per cent, to take refuge in the surrounding farms. The centre of town burned for two weeks. Those who stayed lived in the houses that were left standing, and in makeshift camps.

P.K.: *How did the occupying forces act towards the locals?*

F.L.: They behaved themselves. They were always a little stiff — I'm thinking of the officers in the Hôtel de Paris, where the local Kommandantur was set up, in particular — but for the most part they were good sorts. Even the tall SS chap, Schöllenhammer, who was here for a few months before being sent back to Russia. The Germans paid for what they bought, even their haircuts, as honestly as the rest of us. But the Feldgendarmes would arrest you over the slightest thing, a bald tyre, or breaking the curfew. A constant police presence. They also raided farmhouses occasionally, on the grounds of anonymous letters. But there was no torture or executions. The mass graves that were later found in the forests were the work of the French Gestapo from Rouen and Caen, who spread terror wherever they went, especially when they withdrew in '44 … As the Resistance grew much stronger with all the kids deserting the forced labour service, and as people began to see that the Krauts were on their last legs, that's when a kind of civil war broke out in our country. There was a lot of violence on both sides.

P.K.: *Were the people of Andigny Pétainists?*

F.L.: I wouldn't say that, no. Just obedient to the government, except for a few who openly supported the Maréchal. You know, you won't find much in Andigny - a few people who had their heads shaved after the liberation, but nothing exceptional. Besides, those poor women who got shorn hadn't denounced anyone; they'd just slept with the Krauts. Or not even that — they shaved the head of this young Spanish girl whose only crime had been working as a chambermaid in the Kommandantur hotel! On the other hand, there were a lot of denunciation letters, sent anonymously. Usually to settle personal scores, or to do with land disputes, inheritances … But other than that, the town was quiet. At ten o'clock you had to close your windows and curtains to prevent the bombers from seeing the lights. We lived under the permanent yoke of the Germans. That's all.

P.K.: *Did the Town Council implement Vichy directives?*

F.L.: From the administrative side, of course they had no choice. But as for the rest of it, they were passive. For instance, they had nothing to do with the arrest and deportation of Monsieur Lévy. That started with an article in *Le Journal d'Andigny*, and the Kommandantur decided to act on it. The day the Jew was arrested, I was visiting my mother-in-law who lived across the street, on Rue du Buet. I saw a German truck pull up in front of his house. He was packed off with all his furniture, right up to his fishing rods. They took everything. Monsieur Lévy was sent away because he was a Jew, not because he was in the Resistance. He was a nice man with no family, who wouldn't hurt a fly.

P.K.: *Were there Resistance fighters in Andigny?*

F.L: In terms of action in the town itself, no. I personally joined a group that was blowing up locomotives over by Dieppe. Another local was in a network working out of Rouen. And there were farmers who supplied the Resistance and hid airmen. Monsieur Madry was arrested in '43 with his wife; they sent him to Neuengamme, and her to Ravensbrück.

P.K.: *How many locals were in the Resistance, would you say?*

F.L.: I'd say seven or eight. But then, when I came home after the liberation, the town was swarming with resisters! The truth is, there was never a network in Andigny.

P.K.: *So the Resistance came late to Andigny?*

F.L.: It became active when there was less danger. People were scared for their lives, you know? And then there were those who suddenly discovered towards the end that they had always been resisters, deep down, but that was mostly a desire to be on the winning side.

P.K.: *Was there any violence, or purges, when the town was liberated?*

F.L.: No. People were mostly relieved that it was over. About thirty people went before one of two tribunals: the Court of Justice or the departmental Civic Chamber, but only two or three were fined or sentenced to jail, including the editor of the *Journal*. No one was shot. In other towns, yes, there were cases of summary justice. And let me tell you something: there were a lot more French Gestapo agents than there were members of the Resistance. We hated them with a passion. Later, we were reproached for our excesses; people accused us of taking the law into our own hands. But what were we supposed to do? When we caught a known, registered Gestapo agent with his little yellow card, there wasn't much incentive to arrest him correctly, bring him to justice, wait for the trial and the sentencing. That was too much to ask. We were seething with rage and the desire for vengeance. Our justice was more direct — we kind of settled it on the spot. Those Gestapo agents had a debt to pay, to us more than anyone else. They had betrayed us, denounced us, hunted us, humiliated

us, tortured us, handed us over to the enemy …
They had tricked us by infiltrating our ranks and
then turning us in. How could anyone be expected
to control themselves after that, to abide by
the law? All I could think about was our dead.
So we showed them no mercy.

P.K.: *I read somewhere …*

F.L.: Hold on, hold on, let me tell you another
thing. It wasn't just the Gestapo! Personally,
I consider the broadcasters, speech-makers,
journalists and politicians to have been far
more criminal than the worst Gestapo filth.
Certain speeches and articles, along with the
prevailing climate and 'European' propaganda,
swept men and women into the deadly orbit of
the German police, when their only mistake had
been to swallow everything they heard and read.
Unfortunately, the law courts and tribunals
followed other criteria. They put the torturers
and killers before the firing squad, but those
who had incited them to it usually got off with
a slap on the wrist. To me, that was the real
scandal.

P.K.: *I see … and in what way was the liberation
of Andigny a relief?*

F.L.: Well, they were occupiers after all. So
when they left, people were glad to see them go.

P.K.: *Did the Allied troops stay in Andigny
after the fighting was over?*

F.L.: Yes. The liberators were fêted. But no
one was willing to house the soldiers. You see,
to the people of Andigny, they were foreigners,
too.

P.K.: *So you think the locals just wanted to
draw a veil over the entire period and forget it
all ever happened?*

F.L.: Exactly. People tried to put all the death and suffering behind them. The terrible poverty, too, for those who were worst off. In fact, I was amazed at their ability to forget. All they focused on was getting back to normal. And then, in any case, time passes, doesn't it? It's what you might call natural. The tradesmen gradually returned. It's really pretty around here, as I'm sure you've noticed. The castle, the hills, the Seine … It's a little heaven on Earth. You know, we're really attached to our patch of ground. So all we wanted was to enjoy it quietly …

The following information is drawn from Peter Klemm's documentary *Elsie Bergers Französische Familie*, broadcast on German television in 2008. The film has yet to be distributed in France.

SS Sturmbannführer (Commandant) Hugo Schöllenhammer died on the Eastern Front – in Lublin, southern Poland – on 22 July 1944. Documents found in Leipzig, the officer's home town, include the following extract from the poem 'Ténèbres' by Paul Claudel, written out in the hand of the signatory of the denunciation letter:

> I suffer, the other suffers, there is not any space
> Between her and me, not any word, not any face
> Nothing but the night we share and cannot speak,
> The work-barren night where love is vile and weak.
> I lend an ear, alone, embraced by fear.
> A voice not unlike hers, a cry I hear.

In April 1943, Bernard Grasset published Paul-Jean Husson's latest novel *The Bars of Daylight*, one of the biggest literary successes of the year yet never reissued after the war despite its merits. Arrested at home on 29 August 1944 by the French Forces of the Interior the day after the sub-prefecture was liberated by the troops of the 15th Scottish Reconnaissance Regiment, the writer was held first – to protect him from being lynched by the 'eleventh hour resisters' – at the École Militaire where he had been deputy director during the phoney war, then transferred to Fresnes prison.

On 28 December of that year, he was tried in the Court of Justice.

He was accused of having written viciously anti-Semitic and pro-Hitler articles published in *La Gerbe*, *Au Pilori*, *Révolution nationale*, *Je suis partout*, *Le Journal de Rouen*, and in the local weekly *Le Journal d'Andigny*, edited by a notorious collaborationist; of having joined the Franco-German Committee, founded by Fernand de Brinon, in 1934; of having links with Gustave Hervé, Lucien Pemjean and the authors of a 'long-standing conspiracy against the Republic, aimed at bringing Maréchal Pétain to power'; of having been a financial supporter of Eugène Deloncle's Mouvement Social Révolutionnaire and an associate of Jean Fontenoy; of having participated in the delegation of French authors to Germany in autumn 1941; of having accompanied Lucien Combelle to a French workers' conference in Berlin; and of having frequented the German Institute of Paris alongside Drieu la Rochelle, Henry de Montherlant and Jacques Chardonne.

On the basis of Article 75 of the penal code relative to intelligence with the enemy – which he would use again successfully against Robert Brasillach the following month – the prosecutor called for the death penalty. However, thanks in particular to letters from François Mauriac and André Gide (despite the fact that Husson had openly accused the latter of being a corrupter of youth) attesting to the sincerity and authenticity of his involvement, and to the efforts of his friends in the Académie Goncourt, who awarded their first post-war prize to Elsa Triolet to mollify the Communist Party,[19] Elsie Berger's father-in-law was allowed to plead mitigating circumstances. He was sentenced to fifteen years of hard labour and stripped of his civic rights. He was also struck from the rolls of the Académie Française, like Pétain, Maurras, Hermant and Bonnard. Reprieved in 1952, Paul-Jean Husson returned to live in Haute-Normandie, where he wrote a further four novels, one play and two essays, all unpublished, and died in 1959 in the Trappist monastery at Radepont, near Fleury-sur-Andelle, to which he had retired several months earlier.

In his will, he left 500,000 old francs to Germaine Roussel, née Pin, of Fresne-l'Archevêque – the younger sister of his natural son André Pin.

Olivier Husson entered Paris by Porte de Saint-Cloud on 25 August 1944, riding up Avenue Mozart on a tank of the Langlade tactical group of General Leclerc's Second Armoured Division. As soon as the fighting was over he went to the Eure to retrieve his children and bring them to live with him in Paris. He permanently severed all relations with his father. His efforts to find Ilse Husson – inter alia, among the surviving deportees who assembled at the Hotel Lutetia as they gradually trickled home – came to nothing, and he ultimately believed that she had perished.

He was remarried in 1951 to a musician in the Paris Orchestra. One son was born of the union in 1953.

Omer Aristide Husson became an editor, and in 1982 brought out a collection of his grandfather's unpublished works. Shunned by the critics, the book went unnoticed.

Lieutenant Gerhard Heller, of the Propagandastaffel's Schrifttumgruppe, left Paris on 14 August 1944 in a private car requisitioned during the retreat of the German army. The previous evening, he had buried, in an iron box at the foot of a tree on Rue de Constantine, between Rue de Talleyrand and Rue Saint-Dominique, the journal he had kept throughout the Occupation, in which he had recorded his meetings with French writers and publishers. Years after the war, Heller returned to Paris, but no matter how many times he counted and recounted the rows of trees, he was never able to find the hiding place. He therefore had to rely on memory to reconstruct the document, which was published in 1981 by Éditions du Seuil under the title *A German in Paris (1940–1944)*.

The Gestapo officer Martin Laugnac was arrested on 16 May 1945 at the Danish border after having wandered for weeks through the devastation of Germany. After several months of questioning by the British intelligence and military security services, he was handed over to the French, who had long called for his extradition. He was committed to Caen prison, where he attempted suicide in his cell. The Calvados Court of Justice sentenced him to death, as it had three members of his group previously (two others had been killed by the Francs-Tireurs Partisans in June 1944; another two were captured and condemned to death in the Orne; two more were sentenced to forced labour for life, and the rest evaded justice). Martin Laugnac was shot by firing squad on 15 June 1946 in Caen. Refusing to be blindfolded, he tried to give the order to shoot himself, but the sergeant in charge of the firing squad beat him to it.

Laugnac's direct superior, the man who had trained him, Hauptscharführer Harald Heyns, alias 'Bernard', of the Sipo-SD in Rouen and later in Caen, was arrested in northern Germany by the British in 1945. Summoned before a military tribunal in August 1948 accused of having ordered the executions of Canadian prisoners in Normandy, he escaped shortly before the the trial began by prising off the sheet-metal roof of the courthouse toilets, and was never seen again.

The bodies of the Resistance fighters André Pin and Yvonne Lelouarn were identified in October 1944 among the thirty-eight bodies exhumed from a mass grave in the Lyons forest. Buried just below the surface, the corpses had had their limbs dislocated, twisted and broken, jaws fractured and thoraxes crushed. One of the martyrs had had his lips sewn shut with wire.[20]

Joseph Cuvelier, the erstwhile constable promoted to auxiliary and then 'special detective' of General Inquiries, was jailed in the liberation and brought before the 'Purging Commission' on 26 October 1944. He claimed to have been a member of the Resistance (in the intelligence service of the Mouvement de Libération Nationale). Dismissed from the police force, he was reinstated in 1948 after appealing to the Council of State and with the support of the association of former police officers, which was led by Commissioner Jean Dides, himself a former chief inspector in General Inquiries (in the branch in charge of combating foreign Resistance fighters). Appointed division commissioner, on 17 October 1961 Joseph Cuvelier took part in the suppression of a demonstration by Algerians in Paris and its suburbs ordered by the Prefect of Police, Maurice Papon, and in the ensuing massacres. He retired in 1970.

The archives of the French police concerning the 'Jew-eater', Deputy Chief Inspector Sadorski (first name unknown) of General Inquiries – whose existence is attested to by numerous eyewitness accounts of his arrests – are not open to the public, and the film-maker Peter Klemm was unable to obtain a special dispensation to see them.

Ilse Husson, née Wolffsohn (Elsie Berger), was arrested in Andigny on 5 September 1942 by two officers of the German Gestapo. Following a brief interrogation – in the course of which she was accused of having violated the pre-war census law for German Jews living abroad, and the 1942 regulation on wearing the yellow star in the Occupied Zone – she was handed over to the French police. She was transferred to a cell at Paris police headquarters and then, on 7 September, to the Drancy detention camp. On 6 November 1942 she embarked from Bourget-Drancy station for Auschwitz-Birkenau in convoy No. 42 (1,000 deportees, four survivors). Ilse Husson's pregnancy was apparent to the SS doctor who examined her on disembarkation; along with the children, the sick and the elderly, he handed her over to the camp police. The Schutzhaftlagerführer brought them to a small white building by the camp perimeter known as 'Bunker Two' which was surrounded by Sonderkommando prisoners who, in order to forestall panic, had been ordered to calm the terrified deportees and respond reassuringly to their questions.

SS guards and dogs encircled the building and watched the newcomers, who were informed that they had been brought there to shower and be deloused. Ilse Husson undressed with the others outside the building. Then she was ushered, naked, into one of the four gas chambers, fitted with shower heads and water pipes to allay any suspicion that they were not bathrooms. Bunker Two had a maximum capacity of 1,200 people. The Sonderkommando prisoners stayed inside with the newcomers until the last minute, as did a single SS guard.

After the prisoners and the guard had left, the door through which Ilse Husson had entered was rapidly shut and locked. The 'disinfection' team emptied the contents of Zyklon-B boxes through special apertures. The gas began spreading the moment the pellets hit the ground. Those closest to the vents fell almost immediately. Approximately one-third of the victims died very quickly. The others collapsed upon each other, crying out and gasping for air. The healthy and the young fell last. Their shouts dwindled to moans, and a few minutes later all who had been locked in the chamber were prostrate, twitching ever more feebly. Within twenty minutes there was no movement at all, and having waited an additional ten minutes, the guards reopened the doors.

The naked bodies bore no particular marks; they were neither contorted nor discoloured. There were no lesions of any kind, faecal soiling was rare, faces were not twisted. The corpses were taken from the bunker. The men of the Sonderkommando went to work, opening mouths and extracting gold teeth by means of pliers. The teeth were later melted down by SS dentists into ingots. Ilse Husson had no gold teeth. A prisoner was assigned to cut off her hair, which was later dried in a loft before being bagged and sent to a government factory in Silesia, where it was made into felt or mattress stuffing.

The clothing that Ilse Husson had left outside was collected with the rest and taken by truck to a sorting station. Her naked body was thrown with other naked bodies onto a trolley on a narrow-gauge railway siding. It was shunted to a large ditch excavated outside the camp – this was before the construction of new gas chambers equipped with crematoria – where it was doused in methyl alcohol.

A young SS officer, Oskar Gröning, witnessed the cremation in the ditch. Horrified and shocked, he remained some seventy yards from the flames. A kapo told him later that when the bodies began to burn, gas bubbles formed in the lungs and elsewhere, the corpses seemed to leap, and the male bodies got erections.

Thomas and Marta Wolffsohn vanished without a trace. Their names do not appear on any register of immigrants to Palestine in 1938–1939. Their son Franz, sentenced to death for terrorism, was decapitated by axe at Hamburg prison on 16 October 1940.

Amédée Lévy, the sole Jewish inhabitant of Andigny, never returned from deportation.

NOTES

1 Lieutenant.

2 An office of the Reich Ministry of Popular Enlightenment and Propaganda, with offices at 52 Champs-Élysées. The Schrifttumgruppe ('literary group') led by Lieutenant Gerhard Heller was in charge of publishing.

3 Jean Giraudoux, *Pleins pouvoirs*, Gallimard, 1939.

4 Philippe Pétain, from a speech delivered in Pau on 20 April 1941.

5 An extract from this letter from Philippe Pétain was reproduced in Marc Ferro, *Pétain*, Fayard, 1987, p. 150.

6 By 1944, the Commission had dealt with 666,594 files. In total, 3.1 per cent of the 485,200 people naturalised between 1927 and August 1940 – some 15,154 – were denaturalised between 1940 and 1944. Of the files examined, 78 per cent involved Jews. Between 1927 and 1940, 23,648 Jews (4.9 per cent of the total number of new citizens) had been naturalised. By late August 1943 (when the Gestapo denounced the agreement struck by René Bousquet whereby French Jews were temporarily exempt from deportation), 30 per cent of Jews, some 7,053 individuals, had been denaturalised.

7 Jacques Chardonne, *Chronique privée de l'an 40*, Stock, 1941.

8 The Viking invader Ganger Hrolf, later known as Robert, first Duke of Normandy.

9 See Georges Montandon in *Le Matin*, 5 August 1941, and *Comment reconnaître le Juif?*, published during the Occupation by Les Nouvelles Éditions Françaises, a subsidiary of Denoël that also published *Les Tribus du cinéma et du théâtre* by Lucien Rebatet.

10 Jewess.

11 The three perpetrators, the Hungarian Martinek and the Romanians Copla

and Cracium, were arrested on 19 October 1942 and shot on 9 March 1943.

12 Renseignements Généraux (RG): political security branch.

13 Parti Populaire Français, a right-wing collaborationist group whose leader was the former communist Jacques Doriot.

14 Documents 1 and 2 were filed by France at the Nuremberg trials.

15 Leaders of the National Socialist Party.

16 Name changed. See 'Publisher's Note'.

17 *Sic.*

18 A far-right league of the inter-war period.

19 See Jean Galtier-Boissière, *Mon journal depuis la Libération*, La Jeune Parque, 1945.

20 See Jacques Delperrié de Bayac, *Histoire de la Milice 1918–1945*, Fayard, 1969.

For a list of works consulted and suggestions for further reading, please visit www.gallicbooks.com